Call
for
Obstruction

Call for Obstruction

ANGELS DARK AND DUMB
BOOK 1

Winnie Jean Howard

www.winniejeanhoward.com

ARMLIN HOUSE PRODUCTIONS

Always for Michael
My Heart
My Inspiration

Chapter 1

How did I become the sort of loser who rear-ends a courier van twenty minutes after getting laid off?

Given a choice, I'd spend my afternoon with an extra-large pizza, half a dozen Monsters, and the latest Grand Theft Auto. Instead, I sit in my pickup, parked on the side of the highway, waiting for the other driver to exit his vehicle. Best to size up a guy you've pissed off before meeting face to face. Hopefully, he's an old guy with no will to argue. Luck tells me he moonlights as an ultimate fighter.

Sure, I'm nearly seven feet tall, but thin as a rail and look the part of the quintessential computer geek. My first home is cyberspace. The only threat I pose is to the personal privacy of Internet surfers.

On the passenger seat, under a bag of Tootie Fruities cereal, my cell phone strums like a guitar. I sigh, expecting my mom to be on the other end. But it's not her. The eight-hundred number on my caller ID also bulges out from the van's back door, like in a 3D movie.

Freaky.

I blink and the phone number flattens back onto the van's paint job. I tilt my head and continue to stare, half expecting the digits to pop again. But they don't.

A gruff female voice pipes in over the speaker on the unanswered phone. "OTG Courier Services. How may I help you, Barry?"

I drop the cell to my lap. Eerie enough that the call got through, but how the hell does she know my name? "Hello," I talk down at my lap. "Did you just call me Barry?"

"What, Honey? Barry? Is that your name?" Phlegm gurgles in her throat as if she has a three-pack-a-day habit.

"Uh…yeah."

"Well, Barry, why ya calling?" she asks in a pronounced New York City accent.

I clear my throat. "Um. *You* called me?"

"Why would I call you?" She laughs.

For a second, I contemplate hanging up. Maybe call the police or head down to the county building to file an accident report. Instead I pick up the phone and study the display, as if that will explain how her call got through.

"Hello?" she says. "You still there?"

I rush to reply, "I hit one of your vans and the driver hasn't gotten out—"

A deep hacking interrupts. "Sorry, Honey, I've got the emphysema. Did you say you're calling about a job?"

I hold the phone close to my mouth and yell, "No. I rear-ended one of your vans."

"*Tsk.* I'm not deaf."

"Sorry," I say, then try to sound polite by adding, "ma'am."

"You got a valid driver's license?" she asks.

"Uh huh." I lean over and fumble to pull my proof of insurance out of the glove compartment, assuming she'll ask for it next.

"How about an aversion to heat?"

I push my horned-rimmed glasses back up to the bridge of my nose and frown. My mouth falls open, but I don't answer.

Slow and irritated, again she asks, "Can you tolerate heat?"

My voice squeaks as I ask, "Why? Is your cargo flammable?" I study the door for hazardous material stickers.

"Have you killed anyone?" she asks.

My back straightens against the seat. "I said the driver hasn't gotten out of the van, not that I killed him."

"Don't worry about that one," she says. "Can you come down to the warehouse and sign some paperwork? I can start you tomorrow morning at fifty an hour, if that's enough?"

Fifty an hour to drive a van? This lady must be off her rocker.

I'm done wasting a college degree, achieved by the age of nineteen, on jobs any uneducated schmuck could do. The last three months, working in customer service was torture enough.

"Listen, lady, I'm not calling about a job. I hit one of your vans."

"So what is it, you don't *need* a job or you *need* more money? Because I can go as high as fifty-five an hour."

Dollar signs dangle like proverbial carrots. That and being handed a final paycheck less than an hour ago, a visual of my boss with a forced sympathetic smirk burned into my memory.

"Honey? You still there?"

I raise an eyebrow. "You really want to hire someone who smashed up one of your vans?"

"I need ten new drivers by tomorrow. If you want a job…"

Any way I look at it, I've been laid off four times this year. I have to find a job soon or I'll have to move back in with my mother. A chill rushes up my spine at the thought of it. "How do I get there?"

"We're east of the Denver Tech Center in a red warehouse off Arapahoe and Revere," she says. "Name's Margery. I'm always here."

"What about the van?"

There's silence on the other end as the van pulls forward and merges back onto the highway.

When my phone goes black, a sinking feeling in my gut says get the hell out of here and go file a police report.

I turn the key on my truck and gun the engine. The exhaust backfires like it always does, followed by a cloud of black smoke.

A horn honks. Some guy in a brand new truck with temporary plates zips around me. He flips me the bird.

My hand pauses on the gear shift. Fifty-five an hour would put me in a truck like that. I could be the asshole with the attitude for a change. I shift into drive and merge onto the highway, following southbound to the warehouse.

Chapter 2

THE OTG parking lot's blocked by a couple car carrier semi-trailers. Parked willy-nilly across the lot are a dozen or more new OTG vans. Hopefully a sign that the company's doing well, and this job will last longer than a month. I park on a side street and jog through the mayhem of vehicles to the entryway.

My phone sounds off near the office door. I clench my teeth. This time it *is* my mother. It's like she has a sixth sense about me wasting all the money she spent on my private college education. The fact that I acquired a Computer Science degree by nineteen burns a little more with each unskilled job I take, and lose. How can her smart boy be such a loser?

My finger swipes hard against the surface to ignore her call, but she always tries twice. After counting to ten in my head, the device announces another incoming call from Mom. Only this time the screen blacks out after the first ring. I press the power button. No response despite the half-charged battery. Why argue with good timing? I put the phone in my pocket and step inside the OTG lobby.

The place is deserted even though Margery said she's always here. Her office is nothing like the typical delivery drop-off site. Reminds me a little of my grandmother's basement, or a time warp into the nineteen-seventies. Wood paneling, windowless walls, and dark brown cabinets along one wall make the room eerie despite the florescent lighting.

The empty liquor bottles scattered across an olive green countertop and beside the color-coordinated refrigerator could explain her confusion about the accident. The smoke rising from an ashtray on a nearby table tells me she's prone to bad habits. Who am I to complain? My other bosses this year run stiff competition for worst manager of all time.

"Barry, you made it," says a now familiar voice that seems to come out of nowhere.

I jump, turn, and look downward. A hunchbacked crone with flaming red and orange streaked hair stands behind me. Either she's light on her feet or a magician in her spare time. Her hairdo's combed upwards, like a troll doll, lifting her height to nearly five feet. The woman sure likes orange. It's also the color of the leggings below her blue oversized Broncos t-shirt.

She holds out her hand. "Margery." We shake and electricity surges up my arm. When I stumble backward, she lets go. A crooked smile turns up one side of her puckered mouth and she winks. "You find the warehouse okay?" Her breath packs a punch that smells like raw hamburger rotting in an ashtray.

With eyes popped wide from the lingering electricity, I nod my head.

She points toward the table and leaves me standing in the middle of the lobby. I follow, stroking my vibrating knuckles.

At the table, a chair slides out and hits my leg.

I pause.

The last half hour replays in my head: a strange van, an unexplained phone call, and now the furniture moves on its own.

I should have followed my first instinct. I should have gone home.

I peer across the table to tell her I'm leaving.

Margery's charcoal eyeliner spirals around a bloodshot gaze. She draws me in like a tractor beam. In a slow, hypnotic hum, she says, "Have a seat."

I flop into the chair, but not of my own free will. Set in front of me is a foot-high stack of paper that wasn't there a few seconds ago. I open my mouth to ask about it.

Margery shushes me and reaches for the remnant of the still smoldering cigarette in the ashtray. She holds it between her thumb and index finger, places it between pursed lips, and inhales deeply. The cigarette crackles and snaps until it fires against her skin. When there's no more smoke to draw in, she drops the butt into the ashtray and tamps her thumb down on the red-hot tip. The aroma of tobacco mixed with burning flesh fills the air.

"Before you can work for us"—she pauses to lick ash off her blackened fingertips with a serpent-like tongue—"you must agree to a few employment terms and sign our standard contract. All our drivers sign one."

Bile rises to the back of my throat. I swallow hard and point at the tall stack of paper. "The contract seems excessive. What's in it?" *Not that I'm going to sign it.*

She falls back in her chair, lifts her arm, and a newly lit cigarette appears out of nowhere. "Top copy's salary, fifty-five an hour plus time-and-a-half overtime. There's other standard stuff for liability and such." She flips her hand as if the latter part is unimportant.

My eyes open wide at the thought of making more an hour than any job I've ever landed. But I don't like that this lady can make me sit like a trained dog. I slide my chair back, ready to get up and leave, and at the same time wonder what sort of liabilities require that much documentation.

"Driving for us or any courier service can be dangerous, among other things," she says, as if she heard my thoughts.

"Are you talking about accidents? Are these like insurance forms?"

"Sure." She picks up the pen and holds it out. "Like insurance forms."

I rub the back of my neck and watch her wave the pen like a pendulum. "So if anything happens to me, I'll be taken care of?"

"Yeah, Honey. We'll take care of you." That creepy grin curls up one side of her mouth again.

As much as I'd like to get the hell out of here, this job's salary will keep me independent, not to mention buy me a new computer. Hell, I would sell my soul rather than move back in with my mother. My chair slides back up to the table with no effort from me.

"Right there at the bottom," she says. "Sign your name and you're employed."

My eyes fix on the nib as it continues to sway left and right. In the background, Margery duplicates into two hovering heads, then three, then four. The more she multiplies, the blurrier my vision, until all the colors turn to blackness.

* * *

"All done," Margery's voice echoes in my head while the room comes back into focus.

"I signed?" Smoke belches out of my mouth. I jump to my feet and the chair screeches across the floor. "What did you do to me?"

She stands and pulls the tall stack of papers to her side of the table. "Be here tomorrow morning at six o'clock sharp."

"I don't think so." More smoke escapes my mouth and clouds my vision. I turn around, full circle, and find I'm wasting my breath. There's no one left in the room but me.

Chapter 3

Damn. It's 4:40 in the morning and I'm wide awake. Only birds and insomniacs are up this early.

No longer able to fight the urge to take a leak, I roll out of bed, rub the crust out of my eyes, and shuffle down the hall to the bathroom.

Minutes later, I turn away from the toilet, scratch my protruding ribs, and head for the kitchen to fix a bowl of Tootie Fruities. Cereal in hand, I collapse down on my rock-hard couch. It was a college graduation gift from my mom. She calls it a divan, and it's uncomfortable for a reason. As in 'Don't get too settled in your apartment, Son. Your place is with me.'

I reach over an empty pizza box for the TV remote. It rings and vibrates in my hand. My heart skips. When I realize it's my cell phone, I juggle and it drops to the floor. How'd my cell get here? Last I remember it was on the bed stand.

My nostrils flare as I pick it up and read the eight-hundred number for the warehouse on the display.

Margery's wasting her time. I have no intention of working for her, let alone driving one of her damned red vans. I tap the screen to ignore the call, but the phone continues to ring. The power button is just as unresponsive. I fumble to remove the battery. Still it rings.

Under normal circumstances I'd complain to my cell provider about the phone's malfunctions. Not sure how they'd respond to "How do I stop an old hag from enchanting my phone?"

"Shut up!" I call out.

"Barry?" Margery says through the phone's speaker.

I jump backward on the couch, kick up one foot, and whack my shin on the corner of the glass table. "Shit," I call out, then cuss some more in my head. While I rub the throbbing welt, my eyes transfix on the glowing surface of the cell phone.

"Honey, I can hear you breathing." Her voice transforms from cranky-old-lady to a slow baritone. "Get your ass to work."

I hold myself tightly in place and blurt out, "I'm sick."

"Oh, Honey, I'm so sorry to hear you're under the weather. What's wrong? Got the flu?"

If only she sounded sincere. "Food poisoning," I say. Instantaneously, my stomach churns and gurgles. I rub my palm center-torso and wonder what the chances are of the cramps being a coincidence.

"Tell me it's not the diarrhea," she says. "I hate the diarrhea."

"Been up all night with it," I lie. My bowels growl like a Rottweiler.

"Well, Honey, I'll tell you what." She pauses to cackle. "Come on down to the warehouse, and I bet your *food poisoning* goes away in a hurry."

I lean to one side and pass a long audible wave of burning gas that turns damp. "This is not funny. I'm in a lot of pain here."

"Seriously, I guarantee a trip to the warehouse will fix ya right up," she says. "Besides, I know where you live. If I have to send someone after you, it'll be much worse than a little Montezuma's Revenge."

Chills travel up my spine and my bowels loosen further. I groan, jump to my feet, and run for the toilet.

Chapter 4

BY THE time I walk through the OTG office entrance I'm ten pounds lighter, but like Margery promised, my gut calms.

On the far side of the lobby, fifty or more couriers crowd around a bulletin board. It's like standing outside a mosh pit, watching them slam and elbow each other while they reach for clipboards and keys.

"No announcements!" Margery's voice rumbles like thunder over the throng. "Get on the road!"

After a momentary hush, everyone scatters as if Margery has her finger on a fast-forward button. No time to meet my new coworkers before the sheep push me out of the way to get out the door.

I'm left behind with Margery and a fifty-something guy with a bad comb-over. They stand beside the table where I signed that contract yesterday. I flash back to the moment of the black out and shiver.

"You." Margery wiggles her wrinkled fingers my direction. "Where's my coffee?"

"Coffee?" I say. "I didn't know coffee delivery was in my job description."

"What did you just say to me?" She leans forward with one hand on her hip, puffing hard on the cigarette that hangs from her lip, ash falling to the floor. A heatwave spreads across the room.

I swallow hard and my voice rises in pitch. "Seriously, is it in my contract, because I'll go get—"

The old guy interrupts. "This must be the new kid." He's got one hand in the pocket of a khaki outrigger jacket. His other hand holds a fat cigar stub, which emits the pleasant aroma of fresh cedar. "How's the diarrhea?" he asks while he combs greasy strips of black and gray hair over his clammy scalp.

My face turns red. Now's the time for a snappy comeback, but nothing comes to mind. For once in my life, it's probably better to keep my mouth shut.

Margery's head snaps to the old guy. With a twitch, she pulls the cigarette from her lips and points it his direction. "Vern, get the hell out of here."

Vern holds up his hands in defeat and backs away.

Margery turns to me. "Lighten up, Honey. You're not the first driver to fake an illness to get out of working for old Margery. Some of you idiots even try it a couple times before you wise up. You're not an idiot, are you?"

I shake my head, although getting fired from another job is now high on my agenda.

She motions for me to follow her toward the bulletin board, where she unhooks a set of keys and a clipboard. She throws them at me, and I manage to catch them both. "Let's get your van signed out and get you on the road to Trinidad." She pulls a pen out of the air and shoves it at me.

I hesitate to take it, afraid to put my name on anything Margery presents.

Her finger taps on the clipboard beside an empty signature block. "Honey, you sign or spend the rest of your day in the bathroom."

After a long exhale, I take the pen and quickly cross the letter 'X' on the page: a fool's attempt to escape her trickery.

Margery takes off toward the door, and I chase after her to the back lot, where only three vans remain. She opens the door on one of them and sweeps her hand at the cab. "Go ahead, get in and start it up."

I jump behind the wheel and turn the key. The motor purrs, and the interior has that new car smell.

She points at the passenger seat. "That map will get you to the warehouse in southern Colorado, near Trinidad. Drop off your cargo and come back here." Then she turns to leave.

What, no GPS? And considering the size of my employee contract, I expected her to have more to say. I lean out the door and call out, "That's my training?"

She stops and turns. "Guess I forgot to warn you about the man-sized birds that attack the vans. Otherwise, you're a smartass, you'll figure it out."

My eyes bulge. There's the catch. "What do you mean, man-sized birds?"

Margery jogs away and hollers out, "Like I said, you'll figure it out."

Chapter 5

Two HOURS south of Denver, I feel as though I've been on the road half the day. Even fifty-five dollars an hour can't make up for this much boredom. I've thought about ditching the van, but every time I do, I let out a dusty fart.

An unmistakable hacking cough echoes throughout the cab. "Margery?" It's like she's in my head, but not in my head.

"Yeah, Honey, it's Margery."

I jump in my seat and look around. "Where the hell are you?" A light on the radio catches my eye. It flickers like it's on the fritz. Is that the source of her voice? I turn the only knob on it, but it doesn't seem to do anything.

"Wanted to let you know a few of the drivers have encountered a flock of those birds I warned you about. They're just south of Pueblo. Close to your current location."

"Those things really exist?" I shift in my seat and look skyward.

"Why would I warn you about something that doesn't exist?"

"I'm not a zoologist, but who would take man-sized birds that attack speeding vehicles seriously."

"If you're finished, Mister Smarty-pants, you're in one of the new vans. The damage should be minimal."

"Damage?" I squeeze tight on the steering wheel and talk at the radio. "Wouldn't it be better to get off the highway? Wait for them to clear?"

Her voice fills the cab. "You'll do no such thing. You'll get that cargo to Trinidad ASAP."

"It's my first day." My heart races faster.

"You have two options." She lets out a long sigh that's more of a growl. "Keep on the road or hide in a gas station restroom and shit out your intestines."

Something tells me I'll shit my pants either choice I make. I mumble, "Bitch."

Considering today's been nothing but clear blue sky, I doubt the white mass off to my right is a cloud. It enlarges as it descends. "I think I see them."

"And they see you, Honey."

"I'm not ready for this."

"Too bad," she says. "Keep it on the road and don't stop. They can't hurt you unless you stop."

With wings that flap at a twelve-foot span, the birds swoop in. The first one dives straight at the windshield and hits the passenger side like a cannon ball. At least twenty more dive-bomb behind it.

The van rocks and swerves, but miraculously none of the birds break through.

I lean forward in my seat and hover over the steering wheel, struggling to keep the van on the road. My chin trembles. "This isn't happening."

"It sure is, Honey."

"Stop calling me Honey."

Margery hacks a laugh so hard she could hyperventilate.

"Shut up. This is not funny." I floor the gas pedal, not that this van could outrun them, but it's worth a try. "*Shit!* This is *The Birds* movie on steroids."

"Stop talking and concentrate or you'll end up bird feed." Margery continues to bark out directions, but only half of what she says is discernible amid the screeching birds and flapping of wings against the windshield.

My neck whips backward as a ghostly white, human face head-butts the windshield. The monster snarls and punches the glass, which shatters, but just as quickly, the cracks fuse back into one clear sheet.

"They're not birds," I whisper at first, then reiterate for Margery's benefit as loud as my voice allows. "They're not birds."

Outside the driver's side window, another monster has a tight grip on the mirror. It bares sharp teeth and violently yanks at the door handle.

My body tilts to the right. The steering wheel rotates the same direction through clammy hands. "Ah!" I slam on the brakes to force the thing off the van. The vehicle goes into a tailspin before skidding to a stop.

Margery barks like a drill sergeant, "What part of 'keep moving' did you not understand?"

My foot forces the gas pedal to the floor even though my view is obstructed. "I'm trying. I'm trying," I keep saying. I skid back around to head south and somehow manage to drive back onto the pavement.

"Hold it steady," Margery says. "Help's arrived."

"Thank God."

"Honey, God's got nothing to do with this mission."

Darkness descends over the van. A few of the toothy bastards break away, replaced by black wings and deafening squawks from a murder of crows. A pecking and clawing war between black and white commences overhead.

Blood rains down on the windshield, blocking my sight. My stomach turns as I fiddle with the dashboard controls. The wipers come on and jets of blue cleaning fluid squirt onto the gory mess.

The white creatures retreat back into the sky, a black veil in pursuit. Maybe I'm safe, but that doesn't stop the full body shivers or loosen my tight chest. "Margery, help! Can't…breathe. Having…heart attack."

"Don't be silly. You're in shock?"

"*Shock*. This is…not shock." A bead of sweat streams down my forehead.

"When's the last time you were pummeled by a flock of giant birds?"

"Those were not birds." I pound my fist on my chest and white-knuckle the steering wheel with my other hand. "Seriously. Call an ambulance."

"I don't have time for this nonsense. Pull yourself together and finish your run to Trinidad."

There's silence. Margery's gone.

Chapter 6

I BOUNCE IN my seat over an eroded dirt road. Up ahead, there's a log marker that reads 'Bellow's Ranch' across the top. A faded 'No Trespassing' sign hangs on one post and an OTG Courier sign hangs on the other. To the rear of the van, a hazy trail of dust.

Margery was right. Ten minutes after the attack, I could breathe again. Still, my eyes never stop shifting between the road and the sky, sure those flying white bastards are preparing for another round.

Twenty-four hours ago, being fired from four jobs in a year was an all-time low. How is it I dug myself deeper? My only hope is that I find a way out of this job that doesn't involve Margery turning my asshole inside out.

Beyond a patch of pine trees, a weathered red warehouse comes into view. Wild sunflowers and rusty mining equipment surround the building. From the look of this place, OTG could have gone out of business half a century ago.

A garage door lifts. A tall man wearing red coveralls and a long salt-and-pepper braid down his back limps into view. He waves me inside, then stands by like a proud Native American chief in a history book.

I park the van in the garage and get out.

"You're an hour late," Margery says from a doorway on the left side of the garage.

I halt mid-stride. "How'd you get here?"

The tall man approaches. "Margery is everywhere."

I mumble, "No shit."

"Meet Oscar," Margery says. "He's in charge of the vans down here and doesn't know when to mind his own business."

Oscar grumbles and walks away.

"We need to talk, Honey." Margery turns to leave the garage.

I follow and hope she's about to fire me for poor performance, but reaching the Trinidad warehouse in one piece likely qualifies for employee of the month.

We enter a room that's so freakishly similar to the office in Denver, *The Twilight Zone* theme plays in my head. The only difference here is a wall where the entryway would normally be.

Margery sits at her table, also indistinguishable from the one up north. "How do you feel after your first run?" she asks.

I sit down, take in a long breath, and hang my head. "If that's a typical drive, I'm not cut out for this job."

"Don't disappoint me, Honey. I've got high hopes for you."

I lift my head enough to stare down Margery's wrinkled cleavage. Six inches higher, my gaze meets with her spiraling black eyeliner.

My spine snaps to attention. I grit my teeth and fight the urge to speak, but the words come out anyway. "I'll do better tomorrow. Promise."

"Good boy."

Damn her. I turn away and breathe deeply. Mental note. Never look into her hypnotic eyes again. Hell, avoid looking at anything from her waist up.

Margery stands and walks to the kitchen. "You missed the lunch buffet for the drivers. Luckily there's always something around here to eat." She opens a cabinet filled with mini-boxes of Froot Loops, a brand name too expensive for my budget.

I rip open a carton and pour most of its contents into my mouth.

Free meals on top of fifty-five an hour, and somehow it's my favorite food. Nope. Still not worth fighting those white bastards or putting up with Margery and her freaky cigarettes.

Oscar limps into the room and heads for the refrigerator.

"What do you want?" Margery asks.

He pulls out a soda and pops it open. "Thirsty."

"Give Barry a can," she tells him.

Oscar frowns at me. "He will need something stronger when he finds out he is working for the man down under." He opens the cabinet where Margery got the cereal, only now it's filled with hard liquor. He reaches in for a bottle of gin, walks it over, and drops it hard on the table in front of me.

While I'd like to ask about the cabinet of plenty, I'm more concerned about working for 'The Man Down Under.' I want to believe he means we work for an Australian, but it's time I pull my head out of my ass and admit that this is no ordinary job. "I suppose you mean I sold my soul to the devil." I squeeze my elbows tight at my side and chuckle.

"Sharper than he looks," Oscar says.

My chest tightens.

"Had to go and ruin it for me again." Margery throws her cigarette at Oscar as he gulps down soda. The butt hits the can and bursts into a small flame. He bends forward and jerks the can away from his face. Bubbles spray from his nose.

Margery flips a new cigarette out of the air and points it at Oscar with intent. "Get your ass out of here, or your eyeballs will be the next thing to come out of your nose."

Oscar coughs while he limps out of the room.

I push on my breastbone and count the rapid heartbeats. I want to run, but more than that, I want to know the truth.

I turn back to Margery and ask, "Did I sell my soul or what?"

"You can't just sell your soul anymore. No one's been able to do that since the end of World War II." Margery's eyes roll back like she's dreaming. "Those were the days. Everything was so much simpler back then."

"But you admit the devil has something to do with the contract I have no memory of signing?" I reach for the bottle of gin and remove the cap.

"Well of course, Honey. Difference is you signed over your human life to serve Satan on Earth."

"What the heck does that mean? Serving Satan on Earth." I pause to catch my breath. "Am I some kind of slave?"

"Oh, Honey, it's not that bad."

It's not that bad? I lift the bottle to my lips. She's nuts.

"Yes, it may sound nuts, but seriously, it's not that bad a deal."

I squeeze the neck of the bottle and take a long swig. Smooth at first, with an after-burn that's less jolting than the realization that Margery could be reading my mind.

As the bottle drops to my side, liquor splashes onto my hand. The juniper aroma begs me to numb my fears a little faster. Another sip builds up my nerve to ask, "Exactly who are you?"

"That would take days to explain."

I jump back in my chair and shiver. "Are you Satan?"

She barks out a laugh. "Of course not, although the mistaken identity happens quite often. I suppose I'm flattered that you new drivers would consider old Margery the ruler over all of Hell."

Margery carries on as if I care about her demonic world. "Satan, or The CEO as he prefers we address him these days, has no time for us minions. I've been working for him on Earth for over three-thousand years now and still haven't met him."

"You expect me to believe you're three thousand years old?"

"Demons like me are much older. Like I said, I've been working for The CEO here on Earth for a few millennia. Before Earth, I was the only demon who had worked in every level of Hell. I'm a certified expert in human vices. Coming here was a natural progression for my career."

I get up and pace behind my chair, taking half a swig of gin at the thought of demons having careers.

"Honey, we like to indulge in our vices around here, but take it easy. You've got to drive back north."

I turn to face her. "Can't you snap your fingers and make me sober?"

"I'm a demon, not a witch. You won't enjoy what I'll do to sober you up."

"What, a little fire and brimstone up my ass?"

Margery's voice deepens and her eyes blacken. "Give me that bottle and sit down." She throws a cigarette and the cherry tip hits my chest but bounces off.

My knees go weak. One of my legs lifts and awkwardly steps forward as if a marionette string is attached to my foot. When I try to take another mouthful of gin to calm my nerves, my arms spread outward. "What are you doing to me?"

Margery answers with one of her crooked smiles.

One involuntary step after another, I return to my chair. Margery controlling my body is even scarier than the possibility of her reading my thoughts. The unseen force pushes me down into a seated position. Against my will, I slide the gin across the table.

"Now. Where were we?" she asks.

I fall back into the seat in defeat. "You're a demon, thousands of years old. I'm a slave to Satan, who prefers we call him The CEO. Oh, and it's really not that bad a deal." I timidly turn up a toothy grin.

"Careful, smartass. I can make your life miserable if that's the way you prefer to play this."

Because you're not already making me miserable.

Margery raises her voice. "Like I was saying…when you signed the contract, you may have signed over your human life to work unconditionally for The CEO, but in return you get immortal life, a decent salary, and just about any other nasty little thing your heart desires. A pretty good deal if you ask me."

"What if the only nasty thing I desire is to get out of my contract?" I hold myself stiff in my chair, expecting she won't let me off lightly for speaking my mind rather than just thinking it.

Margery's nostrils flare. She takes a long drag on her cigarette. The tip sizzles and glows brighter. Ash falls to the table. She exhales black smoke that floats my direction.

Waving my hand doesn't dissipate the long stream. It wraps around my throat and tightens. I grope at my neck to loosen the stranglehold, but nothing's there. Burning heat penetrates my skin and travels over my tongue. As my mouth fuses into one immovable muscle, I moan and wish for the days my smart mouth only got me fired.

Across the table, Margery's wrinkles are like elastic and mutate into a scaly, snake-like texture. Her muscles grow as burly as the Incredible Hulk. It clicks why she wears stretchy pants. Thankfully her clothes stay on as she grows over seven-foot tall.

A high-pitched screech escapes through my nose when her hair transforms into real flames. Black horns pop out of her head and sparks spray around the room.

I try to flee, but I'm paralyzed.

"I'm through being nice." Her voice gets underneath my skin like a million fingernails across a chalkboard. Then, all at once, I piss my pants.

Margery howls with laughter as she backs away and deflates into a wrinkled old lady. She sits back down, lifts her feet up onto the table, and takes a moment to puff down half a cigarette.

Whatever spell she put on me begins to wear off. My lips return, but I have to struggle to unstick my tongue from my left cheek. I feel like I'm ten years old again, being put in timeout.

Finally, she speaks. "The CEO owns you now. And he gives me the power to do *anything* necessary to keep my couriers in line. Understand?"

"Mmwa," I say and the rest of my tongue releases. I open my mouth to ask a question but pause.

Margery glares at me. "Careful, Honey."

I guard my face with my hands and shake my head. "I just wanted to ask what World War II has to do with any of this. Why can't you just sell your soul anymore?"

"After all the years of supervising this project, you're the first with the guts to ask that. Then again, no one except Vern and Oscar have had the guts to talk back after the first hit from one of my cigarettes." She turns up one of her creepy grins. "Yes, I do have high hopes for you."

Just my luck, out of all the bosses I've had this year, I impress this one.

Then she adds, "I suppose it won't hurt to tell you that Hell filled up around the end of World War II."

I frown. "How could Hell fill up so quickly?"

"Life was horrible back in the early twentieth century. You humans would sell your soul for a piece of chocolate."

At least they got something tasty out of it. I cover my mouth with my fist and clear my throat, still wondering if she can read my mind. But she appears to be too lost in her story to care what I'm thinking.

"None of us demons estimated the number of souls that would flood in during the world wars. There was a rush to find places to put them all. The CEO had to conjure up a refugee camp for the misplaced souls, which has grown to unmanageable numbers."

"What about God and religion and forgiveness?"

"Ha. Good one. Forgiveness only works when you humans believe you're worthy of it. Most don't." Margery takes her feet off the table and leans forward. "And the CEO kept his mouth shut when God gave Moses those Ten Commandments. He knew you humans would break them, every one of them."

Not wanting to have a philosophical discussion with a demon, I change the subject. "What does all this have to do with our mission around here?"

"Honey, if you read your contract, you'd know that it's all laid out in section two-thousand-twenty."

Read my contract? I cross my arms and glare at her. "And…"

"We're opening the Gates of Hell to release the refugee camp onto Earth."

My arms drop and so does my mouth. "Are you serious?"

"Listen, Honey, you wasted too much of my time with your smart mouth." She jumps to her feet. "I've got a meeting in Hell in about two puffs of my cigarette."

"Wait a minute. You can't leave. We haven't talked about those giant birds," I say, then mumble, "that aren't birds."

Margery points at my wet crotch and grins. "The only thing you need to worry about right now is the mess you've made of yourself. Go to the garage and ask Oscar to show you to the showers. There are coveralls in the lockers. He'll get you back on the road to Denver."

"You can't leave. What if they attack again?"

"No reason to fear the white warriors. They won't attack an empty van on the return trip." She rushes to the door off the kitchen, but turns back before she goes through. "Don't forget my coffee tomorrow." The door slams behind her.

Maybe she's confident I'll get home safe, but who knows what else is out there waiting to take me down? Which is why I rush to the cabinet of plenty and grab two pints of gin. If I do make it home in one piece, I'll drown my regrets about the last few days in *her* liquor.

I head for the garage to find Oscar.

Chapter 7

THE NEXT morning, my eyes pop open at 4:40 A.M., same as yesterday. A dampness between my legs has me on my feet, wondering if Margery can torment me in my dreams.

Then I realize it's milk. I fell asleep eating a bowl of Tootie Fruities cereal and watching reruns of Sanford and Son. As I stretch, pastel colored rings fall off my jeans and onto the floor. What a freakin' mess, but cleanup will have to wait. There's got to be some way out of Margery's contract, and the sooner I get to the warehouse the sooner I can figure it out.

After a long, hot shower, I exit the bathroom rubbing a towel over my head. Off to my right, there's an open instant message window on the computer screen from Nina. We worked together earlier this year, testing software that screws people out of extra insurance premiums based on their health history. Ironic that she still works there because I was doing both our jobs back then. She'd visit my cubical wearing a short skirt, sit on my desk, and swing her shapely legs. Then she'd beg me to finish her testing so she could go home early. I still do whatever she asks. I can't help myself. I'd do just about anything for her.

My heart skips when a new message from Nina pops up.

Nina: Barry Bear, you there yet?

She only calls me that when she wants something.

Barry: Yep.

Nina: Where you been?

I pause and think about telling her about Margery and my mission to open the Gates of Hell, but I don't. She'd only laugh at me.

Barry: Why you on IM so early in the morning?

Nina: Software install. Still waiting to test.

Barry: Bummer

Even though I'd give anything to be in her shoes.

Nina: Well??? Where you been???

Damn, she's not giving up.

Barry: Started a new job. Hate my new boss already.

Nina: Call in sick and take me to lunch. :-)

My heart pounds hard until she adds.

Nina: I wish. Probably stuck here for days.

Barry: Gotta go. Work starts early.

Nina: Bye. Miss you! :-(IM me tonight.

She must need a huge favor because Nina is almost always busy in the evening.

I walk away from my computer and get ready for another day in Hell, literally.

* * *

On my way out the door, my phone rings. It's Margery. I think to ignore her, but know that won't do any good. "I'm on my way," I say without bothering to answer the phone.

"You're learning," she says, followed by one of her annoying cackles.

My grip tightens on my phone. "What do you want?"

"Don't forget to pick me up a coffee."

"I know," my voice irritated. "You told me yesterday."

She clears her throat. "I guess you choose your lessons."

"Sorry." I flip the phone the bird.

"Don't get any of that Starcrap or whatever they call it. Stop at the Purgalator. It's a block before the warehouse. Tell him you're picking up for Margery."

"Purgalator? There are only warehouses and office buildings on that block."

"This early in the morning, do you really want to question a demon who hasn't had any coffee?"

My heart skips. "No, no. I'll find it."

Chapter 8

Sleigh bells on the Purgalator's door announce my entrance. The pungent aroma of dark roast assaults my nose. A bitter brew for the bitter bitch.

The rising sun shines through the storefront window and dim fixtures barely illuminate the shop. Except for the coffee jerk behind the counter, the place is deserted.

The guy drops a rag onto the butcher-block counter and dries his hands on the dirty apron hanging below his Metallica t-shirt. He's sporting a nose ring, earlobe plugs, and black and gray tattoos up his arms. By the look of him, he and his band headline in his mother's garage.

The guy leans over the counter and smirks. "Can I get you something?"

I walk between tall oak tables to reach him. "Picking up for Margery?"

His posture stiffens, like he's been whipped across his back. He skips to the end of the counter, grabs a tall capped-off cup, and rushes to return to the cash register. His hands shake as he places the cup down. "Five twenty-five," he says.

My eyes widen. "She expects me to pay?"

"Trust me, you *do not* want to show up without her coffee."

"Bitch better pay me back," I mumble and reach into my back pocket. The cost of her drink is probably more than the total cash in my wallet.

Sleigh bells sound off, announcing another customer. The coffee jerk's eyes pop and he turns up a toothy grin.

I peer over my shoulder. Too gorgeous to notice a guy like me is the first thing I notice about the woman approaching us. Messy though, dressed all in white with tan, sculpted legs stretching out from under her wrinkled miniskirt. Her blouse is only partly tucked-in and her long brown hair is tousled up into a clip. She looks as if she's on a walk of shame.

"Morning, Trisha." The dirt bag ogles her chest while he asks, "In for an espresso boost this morning?"

"Going to be another hot one today, Harvey. Think I'll have a frozen cappuccino, like yesterday."

Now I get it. She bounces on the balls of her feet while she speaks, and she's not wearing a bra. A welcome distraction from her whiny, high-pitched voice, which failed to mature past the age of five.

"One minute," Harvey says to her. Then he turns back to me with a smirk on his face and his palm held out to demand payment.

I dig into my wallet, reach in for my last five, but instead pull out four crisp one hundred dollar bills. "What the…" I frown and smile at the same time. I haven't had this much cash in forever. I suspect this is my pay for yesterday's courier run, but tell Harvey, "I don't know where this money came from."

Harvey reaches over the counter and snatches a bill out of my hand. "You must be one of Margery's new guys," he says while counting out change from the register.

"Margery?" Trisha backs away.

I hate to admit that this is an all too familiar reaction attractive women have around me. In this case, Margery's obviously the offensive one. Even so, I give them a dirty look before reaching for the coffee and change.

"Good luck," Trisha says. She and Harvey burst out laughing.

Not wanting to be a part of their inside joke, I push open the door and let the noisy sleigh bells announce my departure.

"Tell Margery, Trisha says hi," she calls after me.

Chapter 9

DRIVERS GATHER around the OTG office, only a few recognizable from yesterday. No one returns eye contact. It's easy to understand why they only care about themselves. I have no interest in making new friends either.

"Honey!" Margery calls out from where she sits at her table with Vern. "You made it today. On time even." She looks happy to see me, but only for the coffee. Hope she doesn't expect this to be a daily delivery service.

"Hey, kid, no diarrhea today?" Vern laughs and Margery joins in.

I grumble, agitated I'm the butt of his joke this morning. Walking across the room to deliver Margery's coffee, I resist the urge to throw the steaming brew in Vern's face.

Margery stands, takes the cup from my hand, then yells across the room. "Everyone, get your vans signed out and stick around! I've got an announcement."

Instead of joining the other drivers, I tell her, "Some girl named Trisha over at the Purgalator says, 'Hi.'"

Margery spits out coffee with the force of a firehose. A shower of hot liquid splatters on my face and shirt.

"Damn." I wipe my face on the shoulder of my t-shirt.

With one hand in his pocket and a cigar in the other, Vern shakes his head and walks away. The rest of the room goes silent.

Margery leans forward with one hand on her hip and bobs her head while she speaks. "What did you just say?" Her orange hair is frozen in place like a helmet.

My voice rises in pitch. "Some girl at the coffee shop. She said to tell you—"

Her nostrils flare as she snaps back, "I heard you the first time."

"Then why'd you ask?" After yesterday's torture session I should think before I speak.

Margery rushes me. With each word, she darts her cigarette. "You. Stay. Away. From. Her. You. hear. me?" Holes scorch through my t-shirt even though she's not touching me. Blisters pop up one after another. I cover my chest and turn my back to her. The pain nearly drops me to my knees. "Okay, okay."

I hurry away from her throwing range and blow on my chest to cool the heat. Five minutes into my second day and she's already on my case.

By the time I reach the bulletin board, the blisters are gone, but the burning sensation remains. Why would she let me off that easy?

The same clipboard as yesterday has my name on it. I sign the sheet with my true signature today, take the keys, and forcibly push my way back to where Margery stands.

While everyone gathers around, Margery smirks and watches over the crowd. "Hurry it up. Our schedule's tight again."

"Shit, overtime," someone whispers.

Margery crosses her arms. "I heard that, and you're right. You're all working double shifts."

The crowd lets out a low moan.

From beside the office entryway, Vern steps forward. "You can't do this to us again."

Everyone steps back.

Margery's eyes turn black and her head pops a few sparks. "Do I have to remind you who's boss around here?"

The room goes quiet.

"For how long this time?" he calls out then mumbles, "Bitch."

"Double run for two of you tonight, and everyone else starts back-to-back shifts tomorrow. Who wants overtime tonight?" She stands on her tippy toes and scans the room for raised hands.

No surprise, no one volunteers.

"Fine. I'll pick two of you," she says. "Vern, since you can't keep your mouth shut, you're number one."

Vern protests by scratching his chin with his middle finger.

Margery ignores him and scans the room with the tip of her cigarette, ready to do her magic on the next unfortunate schmuck. "And…"

I raise my hand. "I'll do it." My gut turns with instant regret for volunteering, but this could get me on her good side, if she has one. She might let her guard down long enough that I can find a way out of my contract. And even if I fail, the overtime will buy a new game unit and a few ounces of pot.

"That's what I like to see." Margery winks. "You two, see me before you leave. The rest of you, get on the road."

Vern and I approach Margery's desk.

"Why'd you have to go and pick me for overtime?" Vern's whole body stiffens. His fists clench so tight his cigar snaps in half. The lit tip falls to the floor. "Besides my seniority, which oughtta count for somethin', I've got a hot date tonight."

Her nostrils flare and blow smoke like a bull. "Your time served around here amounts to nothing when you disrespect me."

The two of them stand head to head. I take a few steps back, not wanting to be a part of whatever punishment Margery might dish out.

"Respect, ha! Where's my respect for putting up with your crap for hundreds of years?" Vern breathes so hard, snots fly out of his nose.

Did I hear him right? Hundreds of years? Not a chance I'll work for her that long. I take a few more steps back and nervously fiddle with the keys in the palm of my hand.

Vern walks away from her.

She steps out from behind her table and shakes her fist. "You get back here. I'm not done with you."

"Too bad." Vern sweeps his hand behind his back. "I'm done with you."

Her face creases with rage while she takes a long drag off her cigarette. She takes aim with the cherry tip and bites down on her serpent-like tongue. The butt flies through the air and hits Vern's back. It bursts into a tiny flame and incinerates, leaving a smear of ash on his jacket.

There's nothing to do but wait for the worst to happen.

"Go ahead. Give me diarrhea, hives, or one of your other special gifts." He throws open the office door, but it swings back closed with greater force. The glass surface smashes into his face. Blood sprays from his nose as he drops to his knees. With his hand cupping his nose, he sways like he might pass out.

Margery rushes toward me, almost like she's floating. "Get on the road!" When she shoves me out of the way, electricity rushes up my spine.

I take off toward the door, but pause beside Vern. At first I recoil from the sight of the blood, then crouch down to help him to his feet.

"Get on the damn road!" she repeats. The door swings open by itself.

"Go ahead, kid." He shakes blood off his hand, then wipes the mess onto his jacket. "I'll be fine."

I hedge my way through the door, expecting it to snap back again, but I get through safely. Outside, I run toward the back lot, dodging the vans as they leave the parking lot. Minutes later I follow them toward the highway, more than ready for a few hours away from Margery.

Chapter 10

A T THE Trinidad warehouse, the garage is empty. Vern and I should be the last to arrive, but the other drivers should still be here?

While I get out of the van, Oscar approaches wearing dirty coveralls and a scowl. "How did you get here so quickly?" He limps around by the back door and examines the exterior.

I shrug my shoulders. "The drive was quiet except for the occasional semi truck nearly running me off the road."

Margery enters the garage and joins the inquisition. "That's the only problem you had getting here?" She disappears around the other side of the van.

I call out, "Where are the other drivers?"

At the front end, Margery reappears with one eyebrow raised. "I was just about to ask you that." She kicks the grill. "You didn't pass any wreckage?"

"Wreckage?" A chill runs up my spine as I join her at the bumper. "What's going on?"

No one answers, but Oscar asks, "Did you see Vern?"

"I told you, I didn't see anyone from OTG."

"Don't worry about Vern," Margery says. "He can take care of himself." She rocks the van like a couple of teenagers are going at it in the back, then turns to Oscar and says, "Van's safe to unload."

"Of course it's okay." Then I go at them once more. "What's going on? Where are the other drivers?"

Again, no one answers, but why would they bother to fill in the idiot new guy?

Oscar points outside the garage door. "Vern is here."

"Told you. Nothing stops him." Margery stares at the van as it screeches to a halt, half inside, half outside the garage.

Vern jumps out and slams the door. "Where's Marge?"

"Get your eyes checked." She grins and crosses her arms. "I'm right here."

"Wasn't the nose enough, you old crow?" Vern wriggles where he stands, his blood-crusted shirt half unbuttoned and sleeves rolled up. He scratches at bright red pustules that cover his exposed skin.

"Old crow. Apparently you need to lose a few more layers of flesh to learn to keep your mouth shut." Margery turns to me and asks, "Or should I tie his tongue in a knot? What do you think?"

I touch my chest and feel a residual burn from pissing her off earlier. A reminder to keep my mouth shut.

"Leave the kid out of this." Vern's focus abruptly shifts from his wounds to the empty garage. "Where is everyone?"

"They're all missing except for you and him." She nods her head my direction.

"Oh hell." Vern rushes toward Margery. "You don't think—"

"Of course I've thought of that," she snarls, "but the white warriors haven't taken more than two drivers at a time since that one time back in the early nineties."

My glasses slide down my nose from the sweat forming on my brow. Now I'm really curious, not to mention worried. Why did I get left behind? I step forward, bump Oscar, and raise my voice. "What's going on? Why didn't they take me?"

All three simultaneously turn to me, each with a deep frown.

I grin and slouch my shoulders, feeling as if I've jumped into a snake pit.

Margery rubs her temples and rushes toward the overhead garage door. "I've got to get new vans and drivers by morning. Eat lunch and get back on the road."

"Hey," I call out. "You can't leave."

Vern punches my arm. "Shut up." Then he points at his pustules. "Unless you want some of these.

Chapter 11

IN THE breakroom, there's a smorgasbord of food set out, enough for an army. Vern shoves me out of the way to get at the hot dogs and beans. I approach the other side of the buffet table and grab a couple mini-boxes of Froot Loops and a pint-sized carton of milk.

Vern sits at a table with his head down. He holds his fork like a shovel in one hand and scratches his butt crack with the other. As I approach, the old man eats faster and pulls his plate closer, as if I might try to steal his food.

"Grow up in a large family?" I ask as I sit down.

"No."

"Raised by a pack of wild dogs?"

"Huh?" Vern looks up and frowns as he shoves half a hot dog into his mouth.

"Never mind." I tilt my head back, pour cereal from the box into my mouth, and then take a drink of milk. The crunch echoes in my head as I fixate on the missing drivers. How could that many of them disappear all at once? If this happened before, what might happen next? And why was I left behind?

After a few more mouthfuls of fruity goodness, I ask Vern, "What do you think happened to the other drivers?"

"Traitors likely took 'em."

"Traitors?"

"Yeah. Marge calls 'em white warriors, but they're nothing but traitors if you ask me." Vern takes in a mouthful of beans then waves the spoon while he adds, "Last time this happened, it was them who took the vans and the drivers."

A chill runs up my spine. "What are those things?"

Vern replies with a burp, "You don't know?" His halitosis isn't nearly as rotten as Margery's, but bad enough that I push the cereal box to one side.

"They attacked my van yesterday, but Margery only said they were white warriors."

"Sorry, kid. I forgot you're brand new around here. Marge only wants you to know enough to use it against you. Those traitors are ex-drivers, recruited by angels' apprentices to stop the shipments, but mostly they piss me off." After gulping down the rest of the hot dog, he wipes his mouth with the back of his hand that's still covered in dried blood.

"Why take the other drivers and leave us behind?"

"They know they can't recruit me," he says. "Guess they figure they can't recruit you either. Or maybe they just don't want you." Vern laughs.

I lean into the table and push it into Vern's gut. "That's bullshit. I want out of my contract just as much as any other courier."

Vern drops his spoon and throws up his hands. He's about to speak when a red head pops around the corner.

"Aren't you done eating? Vans are waiting. You've got five minutes to get your asses back on the road if you're going to have time for double runs." She's gone as quickly as she appeared.

Vern scratches his chin with his middle finger.

"You get some thrill out of pushing her buttons?" I ask him.

"We'll talk later." He points at the door. "You better go, kid, before you end up scratchin' like me."

Chapter 12

THIRTY MINUTES into my second run from Denver to Trinidad, the sky grows darker by the minute. Bright veins of lightning strike at the foothills and rumble with each flash. So far the road's dry, but this sort of cloud always dumps a blinding downpour. A rest stop would be a good place to wait out the storm, but there's also a chance of becoming a sitting duck for the white warriors.

My eyes widen and glue to the side view mirror. To the rear, a funnel cloud reaches down from the sky. It lashes at the air, and the whistle of the wind amplifies.

A hand sprouts from the tail of the tornado. When it points an index finger at my van, there's no question of it being supernatural and out for my blood.

A body tremor starts in my torso and works its way through my limbs. My first impulse is to floor the gas pedal even though I can't possibly outrun the storm. Better option, get off the highway, out of the van, and to lower ground—let it have the cargo. I slam down on the brake, steady the van out of a fishtail, and skid to a stop in the median.

Margery pipes in. "Honey, get out of the van!"

"No shit." I kick open the driver's side door. The whipping wind cracks metal and rips it off the hinges. I hold tightly onto the steering wheel so as to not be sucked out next.

Margery warns me again, her barking muffled by the roaring tornado.

Against the force of the airstream circulating throughout the cab,

I climb to the passenger seat. It takes the force of my entire body to open the passenger side door. I jump out, dive over the guardrail, and roll down a steep embankment. Frantically, my hands grab at anything and everything to slow my momentum. Boulders and branches jab my torso and limbs, and I lose a shoe. When my head smacks against something hard, I'm knocked out cold.

Chapter 13

"**H**EY, KID?" Vern calls from above. "You okay?"

I spit a mix of dirt and pine needles. Overhead, a gigantic blue spruce brushes the back of my shirt. My head feels like someone took a hammer to it.

I tuck my arms and roll out from under the low veil of the tree, every movement a reminder of the acrobatic feats that landed me here. I'll take the pain. It tells me I'm still alive.

Crunching footsteps and chirping birds echo in my head as Vern makes his way down the hill. He hovers with his hands in his pockets. He watches as I grit my teeth and struggle to get back on my feet. I clutch my ribs and groan, then pull a pine needle from my cheek.

Standing higher on the hill, Vern's able to look me in the eyes and ask, "You get caught by that tornado?"

I snicker. "No, I thought breaking every bone in my body would be a fun way to start the second run." I roll my eyes and a sharp pain stabs my forehead. With my eyes closed, I gently rub my fingertips over my temples.

"Be glad you're in one piece." Vern turns to ascend the hill. "Let's go. We've gotta get back on the road."

"Are you nuts? Call for an ambulance." I moan some more for effect. Being in the emergency room, hooked up to torturous medical devices, sounds more appealing than three hours in Vern's van.

"Stop being such a pussy. You're fine." Taking long strides, the old guy sets his pace and leaves me behind.

When I stand up straight, most of the pain is gone. A few hops on my foot tells me it's good as new until a pine needle pierces my heel. It's like the rapid healing this morning, after Margery burned my chest with her voodoo cigarette.

I tread over damp rocks and branches to catch up. "You're right. How is the pain gone so fast?"

"Immortal life ring a bell?" Vern crouches and reaches for my shoe. He throws it over his shoulder.

Without my glasses, I squint to focus on the black smudge in the air, but miss the catch. I use my big toe to turn my shoe over, then shove my foot inside it and rush to catch up. "So that eternal life thing is real?"

"Look how steep this hill is." Vern points at the guardrail. "You never would've crawled out from under that tree if you were still mortal."

"If I hadn't signed my life away, I wouldn't be here either."

"Quit your whining. We need to get at least one load to Trinidad tonight."

As we reach topside, Vern leans over again, this time to pick up my glasses. He hands them to me.

I put them on and ask, "How come Margery's contract comes with immortal life but doesn't come with vision correction?"

"Doesn't cover dental either." Vern opens the passenger side door on his van and invites me inside with a wave of his hand.

The interior smells like cigars, hopefully the source of the gummy coating on the seat. Fast food bags and candy wrappers fight for space between my size fourteen feet. "Don't they clean your van?"

"No one messes with my stuff."

I mouth, "Okay."

After Vern pulls onto the highway, I turn my head to stare at the foothills in the distance.

We travel south in silence for a few miles before Vern asks, "What's your story? How'd you come to sign a contract?"

"I don't know. Hell, I don't even remember signing it."

"No one recollects signin', but everyone's done somethin' to get suckered into servin' Satan."

My mind wanders around the legal fees I cost my mother for hacking a retail store to get free computer equipment. There's also the underage pot smoking. Instead of confessing, I change the subject. "You think a tornado took the drivers this morning?"

He doesn't answer at first, then clears his throat and sits straight and proud. "Can you keep a secret?"

I sigh instead of answer. Sure, I can keep my mouth shut, but any confidence with Vern will likely lead to more trouble.

"Was me." He points to himself with his thumb. "I gave up them drivers."

Apparently silence was an open invitation to spill his guts. Still, he's got me confused. "You gave them up? What's that supposed to mean?"

"I got my hands on the hex Marge puts on the vans. I gave it to the traitors."

"You mean the white warriors?"

He fixes his eyes on me instead of the road. "Yeah, so them bastards could take the vans."

I gasp for air and look around the cab. "Aren't you worried she's listening to our conversation?"

"Nah. She's too busy in Hell, answerin' for what I did today."

This is interesting. Until Vern's run-in with Margery this morning, they both gave the impression he was Margery's pet driver. Now he tells me he's sabotaging her operation. What else is he willing to do behind her back? Like maybe help a guy find a way out of his contract?

"Um…why'd you do it?" I frown and instantly regret questioning his motives. "Then again, maybe you should keep me out of this."

"No, no. You'll thank me when I tell you why. I'm even bettin' you'll wanna help me." He shifts in his seat.

"You've already told me too much, and I don't want Margery reading my mind and blaming me for whatever you have up your sleeve." Right about now would be the perfect time for that tornado to return and suck me out of this mess.

Vern laughs. "You think she reads minds?"

"After a torture session with her yesterday, sure seems like she knew what I was thinking."

"Forget it," he says. "Marge knows how you new guys think, not what you actually got goin' on in your heads."

"Are you bullshitting me?" I clench my teeth.

"She plays that game to freak you out and gain control."

"Why? It's not like her cigarettes and seven-foot 2.0 version don't do that."

"Never mind Margery. I need to tell you somethin'." He's hopping all over his seat again, his eyes drilling into me.

My guess is he'll keep after me until I let him speak his mind. Can I take three more hours of pestering—or two the way Vern drives? "Fine, tell me the rest of your secret."

He smiles and blurts out, "Remember what I told you about the traitors takin' all the vans over twenty years ago?"

"Barely." I sit motionless and brace myself for the direction he's heading.

"It was me who made that happen." Vern pauses to merge into the left lane. "We're real close to opening the Gates of Hell again, and I'm going to stop it from happenin' like I did back then."

I jump to ask, "How close to opening?"

"Weeks."

"Why would you go against Margery and stop the Gates from opening?"

"Simple. Drivers get no special treatment when the refugee camp spills onto Earth. We're damned along with everyone else. I, for one, don't want to pay for my sins. Do you have any idea what they do down in Hell to punish guys like me?"

Figures, Vern's saving the world only to save himself. I give in and play along. "What?"

Vern points at a picture of a cow that hangs from the dashboard.

"You a farmer in your spare time?" I ask even though my imagination says otherwise.

"No," he snaps back. "That's one of my girlfriends."

I cringe through an uncomfortable silence.

Vern finally asks, "You going to say something?"

"I'd rather vomit."

"Hey, maybe I'm a pervert, but Margery told me how you've been hacking computers since you were nine."

"I haven't stolen anything since I was fifteen." Thanks to my mother's constant pestering, not to mention our priest, Father Timothy's Catholic reprogramming. "My vices don't compare with fucking animals."

"I ain't no cow fucker."

"You said she's your girlfriend."

"That ain't how I love my ladies. You ever heard of the cattle mutilations down here in Southern Colorado? That ain't aliens doin' that. I love my girlfriends by carvin' 'em up."

"Vern, that's worse." I swallow hard and fight the urge to kill him.

Again there's a long silence between us; again Vern breaks it. "Listen, kid, I don't care what you think of me. All I care about right now is makin' sure the Gates don't open. So either you're with me or against the world."

"That's not fair." So much for getting out of my contract and getting on with my life. "Can I think about it?"

"No. What's it gonna be?" He glowers at me with a hint of expectation for an answer.

I hesitate, but agree only to get him to shut up. "I guess I can help, depending—"

Vern punches my arm and smiles. "Did you hear that, Marge? The kid's with us."

Margery's hoarse voice pipes in. "Yeah, I heard. Get your asses to Trinidad and we'll talk."

My whole head heats up. I'm an idiot. Of course Vern lied about her being busy in Hell. Of course she was listening in over her demonic speaker system. But why would a demon want to close the Gates of Hell?

Chapter 14

VERN AND I enter the Trinidad warehouse to the usual cold shoulder from Oscar. He stands behind his workbench with his chest puffed out and a screwdriver in his hand. The guy looks like he's ready for a lethal stab. "Margery was called to Hell," he says.

"Did she say why?" Vern throws his keys at Oscar.

With eyes fixated on me, Oscar lifts his free hand and makes a perfect catch. "Something about too many missing drivers, and now the warehouse workers are missing. She wants the two of you to hurry back to Denver and load vans for tomorrow morning."

Vern shakes his head. "I was afraid this might happen." He walks toward the garage exit. "C'mon, kid. Let's go eat."

I follow and whisper to Vern, "What's up with Oscar?"

"We've got worse things to worry about than that weirdo."

"Even if he looks like he wants to kill me?" I glance over my shoulder and spot Oscar standing in the doorway, listening to our conversation. He turns and walks back into the garage.

"He's protective of Margery, but she don't tell him nothin'."

Vern flips on the light switch in the breakroom. Hell's caterers have the usual buffet laid out. I grab a couple boxes of Froot Loops and head for the cabinets along the far wall. My hope, it's supplied with anything I want like the one in Margery's office.

Hot damn! There's a bottle of the gin waiting for me front and center. I reach for it and take a swig, then tuck it under my arm and open a box of cereal. "Mmmm. Gin and fruity cereal."

"Nasty, kid." Vern grabs a plate and heads for the buffet table. He fixes himself a third serving of hot dogs and beans for the day.

I'm nasty? He's going to fog up the van with old guy farts the whole drive back to Denver.

I drop the cereal on the table. The open box tips and spills across the surface. "Crap." I say and fall into a chair.

Vern joins me. "Slow down, cowboy," he says with a mouth full of beans. "This is going to be a long night. We need you at least partially sober."

"Maybe *you* should slow down on the beans, cowboy." I mix Froot Loops and a few swigs of gin in my mouth, chew a few times, and swallow hard. My eyes widen. *Not half bad.*

"What's up with loading vans? Double shifts are bad enough." I yawn. "When are we supposed to sleep?"

"Sleep. You don't need no sleep. I once drove three weeks of nonstop runs and never dozed off once."

My eyes widen. *Shit.* It's like this job is making up for all the time I sat at home and collected unemployment.

"What's the matter, kid? You need to call your mommy and tell her you'll be home late?"

Call. My phone. It's been quiet all day—not normal. I pat my pants pockets and find them all empty. My heart skips as I check them a second and third time. Nothing.

"You lookin' for this?" Vern drops my cell facedown on the table.

"What are you doing with my phone?" My lips flatten as I pick it up.

"After the tornado, I found it on my way down the hill to save your sorry ass."

I press the power button a few times but it won't turn on. I cross my fingers it's the battery and put it in my pocket. "Why didn't you give it back to me then?"

Vern shrugs. "We've got more important things to discuss. Time's a-tickin' and we've got to keep the Gates of Hell closed."

"Yeah, about that, I don't think I'm the right guy to help out."

"Too late," he says. "What do you think Marge will do if you try to pull out after agreein' to help?"

I'm such an idiot. Never volunteer. Never do more than expected. Before this job, my old bosses called me Mr. Slacker, now here I am vying for employee of the month.

"Why exactly does Margery want to stop the Gates of Hell from opening?" I ask. "I understand why you would do it, but she's a demon. Wouldn't it be like going home?"

"If you were born in the slums of New York and moved to a Park Avenue penthouse, would you want to go back to your roots?"

He has a point.

"Where exactly are the Gates?" I ask.

"Out at the Bellow's Ranch, a few miles west of here. It's down airshafts into the ol' coal mines." He pauses to belch. "You can pretty much open to Hell from any coal mine. It's something about the composition. Marge says you'd have to be a physicist to figure it out."

"If the hellhole needs a scientist to explain it, how is an operation like this able to open the Gates, let alone close it?"

"Marge has never been too forthcomin' about the openin' of the Gates. All I know is the cargo we haul comes from all over the country but mostly Chicago. I don't know nothin' about how it's collected, but I do know it's something evil and it's in oxygen tanks. You'll see when we get back north."

"If evil's opening it, I suppose something good will close it?"

"That's somethin' Marge *don't* want you to know." He pushes his plate forward. "But I like you. If you're going to be in on this with us, you need to know the whole truth. Problem is you're not gonna like it."

"We're slaves to Satan and an ugly ass demon." My shoulders slump. "Why would I expect you to tell me anything I like?"

Vern's quick to say, "It's kids." He smirks like he's hoping to piss me off.

Anything that starts with kids and involves Hell is going in the wrong direction. "Kids?" I hold my breath and glare at him before asking, "What do kids have to do with this?"

"We're sacrificin' kids to close the Gates of Hell."

All the muscles in my face melt. "You plan to do what?" My fists clench, ready to jump over the table and kill the bastard.

"It's their energy. Their innocence." Vern stumbles over the rest of his speech. "You remember what it's like to be a kid? They don't have a care in the world. When all their innocence and good energy hits the evil energy in the airshaft, it'll form a barrier. Save the world."

"I'm not helping you do that." I stand, ready to leave the room.

He quickly retorts. "Remember the alternative. You'd rather see all the kids in the world tortured by demons?"

I sit back down, curious about the depths this guy will go to convince me to kill children. And because he's my ride home.

Vern puffs out his chest. "It has to be done."

The sick bastard thinks he's some kind of hero.

"Where are you getting the kids? Not that I'm agreeing to help you." More like figuring out a way to rescue them.

"Thirty years ago I kidnapped the little bastards, snuck onto the Bellow's Ranch, and dropped them into the airshafts. Took months to fill up the hole."

"Margery didn't figure out the hole was closing?"

"No. Well, not until the earthquakes started." He scratches his head and leaves his comb over messy.

"Didn't that seem odd?"

"At the time…no." The confused look on his face shifts to confidence. "But later, when Marge figured out what I did, she wasn't mad. That's when I found out she doesn't want to go back to Hell. She thanked me and even protected me.

"Considerin' she's helpin' this time, it'll be easier to close the Gates. She found plenty of the little shits for sale on the dark web. Mostly they're from Central America. You know, the ones who hop the trains to come into the country illegally." He says it like we're talking about a shipment of Nikes.

"Vern, I'm not helping you kill kids." In fact, I'd rather burn by thousands of Margery's cigarettes than have anything to do with his way of closing the Gates of Hell. "There's got to be another way."

"Maybe, but this is the quickest *and* the cheapest."

"What do you mean the cheapest?" The vein in my neck throbs as I grind my teeth.

He looks straight into my eyes. "They have no future. What we're doin' will save them from a life of misery and poverty."

"You're sick." Again I lean over the table to hit him but stop short. At this point, I blame myself for volunteering for overtime only to end up an accessory to murder. I should swing my fist at my own jaw. "What if we let the kids go and don't tell Margery? Give me a few days to figure out another way to close the Gates?"

"No time for new plans." Vern gets up and heads for the door.

I chase after him. "There has to be another way. I could go talk to an angel's apprentice. I bet they could help."

Vern stops and turns. "As deep as you're into this, they'd take your head before you could say two words. And if they don't get you, Marge'll take your head. Trust me, you don't want to find out what happens to dead couriers."

"C'mon." I resort to begging. "Give me one chance."

"Done deal. We're closin' the Gates with the kids and you're helpin'."

Chapter 15

I KICK OPEN the door to my apartment.

Lived in. Yeah, that's a good description for my place, lived in. Dirty clothes liter the floor like a trail of breadcrumbs. I reach down, pick up a t-shirt, and smell it. My nose turns up and I drop it back down to the floor. The whole room's a visual metaphor for what I've made of my life.

Hell's alarm clock goes off in forty minutes. There's no chance I'll catch a power nap.

I pull my t-shirt over my head and let it fall near the other. I take my cell phone out of my pocket, plug it into the charger, and turn it on. Two seconds later, I step out of my baggy jeans and untied shoes, kick my boxer shorts onto the corner of a bookshelf, and walk naked to the bathroom.

Under the shower, I increase the temperature as high as it will go. The heat scalds my body as if I've descended into Hell, but I'm still cold inside. *I won't be a part of a child sacrifice* reverberates in my head, drowning out all potential ideas to get out of this mess.

Ten minutes later I step out of the bathtub and towel off. In the other room my cell phone announces an incoming call. I pause and consider checking it, but only Mom or Margery would call this early. Mom can wait, and the evil bitch can get her own damn coffee this morning.

I head for the kitchen and grab a handful of Tootie Fruities cereal from out of the bag on the kitchen table. I shove it all in my mouth, reach for my phone, and check for voicemails. Surprisingly, there are no calls from my mother. The only number listed is Nina's. She usually texts me. *Why a phone call?*

My fingers fumble to access voicemail. Nina's voice pipes in. "Bear, why haven't you texted me back?" Her tone's whiny, like a little girl. Always an indication something's wrong. "I guess I'll see you at the OTG office." The message cuts off.

The phone falls from my hand. There's only one reason she's going to the warehouse this morning.

I pick my phone back up, hold my breath, and check the text messages from Nina. There they are, five of them, all mentioning she's been laid off.

Shit! Getting out of my contract will be hard enough, but two contracts?

I speed dial Nina's number and step into the pants I wore yesterday. My heart races so fast, I'm dizzy. Her phone rings while I hurry to put on my shoes and dig my keys out of my pocket. No answer. Finally, the voicemail picks up. "Don't go to the warehouse," I say into the mouthpiece. "Don't sign anything." I end the call and run out the door, then turn back to put on a shirt.

Chapter 16

I JERK OPEN the OTG office door, rush in, and call out, "Nina!"

The heads of nearly twenty new drivers turn. A few of them back away. None of them are Nina. I can only hope she got my message and stayed home.

Margery separates the crowd with a wave of heat. She stares at me with that evil half-grin of hers as she approaches. "What…no coffee for me this morning?"

"Where is she?" I clench my fists and approach the demon bitch.

"Who?" She winks and pulls a cigarette out of midair. Muffled whispers fill the room.

"You know who!" I stretch my neck and scan the crowd, but still no Nina in sight.

Then, the restroom door creaks open and Nina walks out. All heads in the room turn toward her. "What?" she says with a hiccup of black smoke. She touches her lips and giggles like she's drunk.

It's too late. She signed Margery's contract.

I swing around and strike a right hook across Margery's jaw. The crowd lets out a synchronous gasp, more so because she stands firm with her hands on her hips and shows no sign of pain or injury.

I'm lying on my side in a fetal position, clutching my fist between my thighs. Every frickin' bone in my hand feels shattered.

Margery stands over me and wiggles her jaw. "Who knew you could pack a punch," she says, "but you won't do that again now, will you?"

A wide-eyed Nina rushes to my side. Her short skirt billows

outward, revealing her white silk panties. "He needs a doctor. Call nine one one!" She drops to her knees and strokes my leg.

It's the first time she's touched me, and that close to my groin, my body reacts with an instant, noticeable hard-on.

Margery turns to Nina. "As happy as he is to see you, he'll be fine." She yawns and steps away.

I extend my injured hand and use it to hide the tent in my jeans. I howl with excruciating pain, an instant cure to stifle the excitement Nina stirs in me.

Nina helps me to my feet, but I'm still hunched over wincing and cussing under my breath. I grab her wrist with my good hand and squeeze. "Why did you sign the contract?"

Nina tilts her head to one side and opens her mouth to speak. A squeak is all that comes out.

I yank her arm. "You don't understand. You can't do this job." Unlike past occasions, I don't have the time or the ability to keep *this* boss off her back. It'll be a miracle if she keeps her sanity after a white warrior attack. Or maybe they'll take her, and I'll never again have a chance to stare into her beautiful green eyes.

As Nina tries to pull away, her lips quiver. "You're hurting me."

All my breath exhales with a groan as I let her go. I clutch my shattered hand and stand up straight.

Margery calls out to me from across the room, "You."

My head jerks like a trained dog to the sound of her voice.

"In the garage. Now!" She rolls her cigarette between thumb and index finger, a motion I now know means she's serious. "Everyone else, get on the road!"

"Screw you," I mumble but do what I'm told. While holding tightly onto the knob of the door into the garage, I turn back to meet Nina's confused stare. I shake my head, turn away from her, and slam the door behind me.

Chapter 17

Vern's alone in the warehouse, puffing on a cigar beside a canister clearly marked flammable. The guy's *brilliant*. Then again, blowing up Margery's operation would be one way out of this mess.

I glare at Margery while she enters through the retracted garage door. My voice echoes as I confront her. "Why'd you bring Nina into this?"

"Vern tells me you're having second thoughts." She rushes me and grows in size with each step.

"Only because he said you're—"

Vern clears his throat.

I snap my mouth shut. He's right. She's already pissed. Who knows what she'll do if she finds out I know her true plan is to sacrifice kids? Right now I need her off my back so I can devise a plan to save the innocents and nullify two contracts. My body sags at the thought.

Her broad, black demon shoulders hover like a looming shadow as she adds, "Let's call her 'insurance'. You do what you're told and I'll release her to you. She'll be yours to use in whatever way your dirty mind desires. If you interfere with the closing of the Gates, well, who knows what might happen to her."

"You didn't have to do this!" I lunge forward but stop when I try to make a fist. The searing pain reminds me what the first punch got me. I back down, choosing to drive to Trinidad with a healing hand instead of every bone in my body being broken.

"It's time to get you and Vern on the road. Follow me." Margery turns her back to us. She deflates as she lets out a lungful of sulfurous smoke. "You won't be driving vans today."

Vern follows Margery through the overhead garage door to the alleyway.

I hold back at first, then follow to where two white box trucks are parked. Both are unmarked except for stock numbers six-six-six-one and six-six-six-two on the side. *Figures.*

"You're driving these trucks today." Margery hands Vern a set of keys, then dangles the other set off her finger for me to take.

"I can't drive one of those." Not only because I've never driven a big ass truck, but also because the larger vehicles make more sense to haul kids to Trinidad. "I'll go check out a van." I turn to leave.

A cigarette lands on my back and paralyzes me long enough for Margery to say, "You drive this truck or your girlfriend goes to the demon camp on the Bellows' Ranch."

My body stiff, I turn back around and glare at her.

"See ya down south, Marge." Vern grabs my set of keys and pulls me by the back of my t-shirt over to the truck I'm driving. "You really need to learn to pick your battles."

This from a guy who scratched off five layers of skin yesterday for talking back to Margery.

I stumble behind him. "Sorry. Seeing Nina set me off." Then I whisper through gritted teeth, "And I'm pretty damn sure the kids are in these trucks."

Vern's voice drops to match mine. "All the more reason to keep your mouth shut or Margery's likely to contract half your family too."

I step up into the cab, put on my seatbelt, and turn over the engine with my good hand. It'll be a bitch driving a box truck one-handed, especially against whatever the angel's apprentices send our way next. But that's the least of my worries. I have only three hours to figure out how to save Nina, the kids, and myself. If I pull this off, for my next job I'll apply for my own Marvel comic series.

Chapter 18

Just south of Fort Carson, there's a white Mustang parked in the median. A woman wearing a white top and miniskirt stands beside it. Her legs stretch up to her neck, just the way I like them. She waves her arms above her head like she wants me to stop. By now I know better than to trust any clusters of white. I pass her by.

Four miles south, it's deja vu: white Mustang, white skirt, shapely legs. She waves at me again.

For about ten seconds, I consider pulling over to defect like all the drivers who've "turned traitor," as Vern would say. Then I remember what's in the back of the truck and worry I might not qualify for employment as a white warrior with the angel's apprentices.

I speed up.

Not ten minutes later, no coincidence, the same scene greets me up ahead. This time she stands spread-eagled in the middle of the highway, waving her arms above her head. I veer left and press the gas pedal to the floor. Her right arm winds up like an ace pitcher and throws a wide curve ball. In mid-air, the ball inflates into a giant white sphere that soars at the truck.

"Margery," I call out.

No answer from the demon intercom.

My ass cheeks clench and my grip tightens on the steering wheel. "Oh…shit!" The sphere hits the windshield and bursts like a water balloon. White liquid splatters across the glass and blocks the view. I slam on the brake, swerve left, and skid to a stop in the median.

Still unfamiliar with the truck, I nervously fiddle with the knobs until the wiper blades switch on, but the covering is as dry as cement. Not even the wiper fluid will remove it.

What now? A voice in my head says, *run*, but if I stick even my head out the window, who knows what she'll throw at me next? But if I don't get this truck to Trinidad, Margery will take it out on Nina.

The side view mirror reflects the girl in white. She approaches on six-inch heels as if she's an Olympic sprinter.

When I reach for the door handle, ready to jump out and give her a piece of my mind, the door opens by itself. Great, another magician. And I'm pretty sure this one's even less on my side than Margery.

"Come on out," she says.

Afraid of what she might do next, I jump to the pavement and glare at a familiar face. "*You.*"

Trisha, the girl from the coffee shop, smiles and bounces. She brushes brown hair out of her mouth and away from her face. "Hi, Barry."

I'd like to tell her I'd recognize her tits anywhere, but instead I manage, "What the hell did you throw at the windshield? You could have killed me."

She rolls her big brown eyes. "Not likely."

"What are you doing here?" I ask, although there's no question that she works for the heavenly forces.

"Are you kidding? I know what you're hauling in there." She cocks her head and points at the back end of the truck. "Man, have you made some poor choices over the last few days."

"No shit," I mumble. "What are you? One of those white warriors?"

"Do I look like the sort of idiot who would sign one of Margery's contracts?" she says. "Try angel's apprentice. The warriors work for me."

"Really?" My eyes widen. "So that's why Margery burned me with her cigarettes when I mentioned your name."

Her thick lips turn up a grin that might be more evil than Margery's.

"After a millennium, it's good to know I still get under her skin."

"Let me guess, you're the one who turns the couriers, and that's why you're here? To turn me?" A chill runs up my spine at the prospect of becoming one of those flying white bastards under the control of Trisha. That's assuming she lets me live for carrying children to their death.

"Ha." She pokes her long red fingernail into my chest. "Your redemption won't be that easy."

"What happens now?" I hang my head and brace myself for the worst.

"Well, if you cooperate—"

"What do you want?" I perk up. "I'll do anything."

"Careful. Being too compliant is what got you into this mess in the first place." She swipes a bug off my t-shirt. "For starters, tell me why you and Vern are transporting kids."

I'm quick to answer. "Margery's sacrificing the kids to close the Gates of Hell."

Her voice rises in pitch. "And you're helping?" She gets extra bouncy when she's upset.

All I can think to say is, "Only until I find a way out of this."

She shoves me. "For yourself or the kids?"

I crash back against the truck. She's stronger than she looks. "You don't understand. I didn't have a choice."

She pushes me again and again. "You always have a choice. Prayer ring a bell? Why didn't you ask for God's help?"

She doesn't let me answer.

"Your poor mother brought you to church for all those years, and all you do is look out for yourself." She shakes her head. "Father Timothy spent years keeping you out of trouble and you sell your soul. He'll be heartbroken."

Suddenly I feel ten years old again. The uncomfortable feeling in my gut tells me to change the subject. "How is it your side doesn't already know what Margery and Vern are up to? I mean, you know about the kids or you wouldn't be here."

"Margery's a lot more powerful than you might think. Her magical cigarettes are nothing compared to the other tricks she has up those spandex pants. Plus, the warehouses, vans, and ranch are protected by a powerful smoke screen spell. About the only way we get information is from the drivers we capture, and most of them are useless." She pauses to cross her arms. Her long fingernails tap against her elbow. "Every now and then, Margery makes a mistake, like today. Would you be surprised to know there's no protection on the trucks you and Vern are driving? The angels saw the cargo as soon as you both drove out of the parking lot and sent me."

I slap my hand against the truck. "She must be distracted because the Gates of Hell are ready to open and she wants them closed." Listen to me, making excuses for a demon who delivered me to her enemy.

"And you didn't think to tell me the Gates are opening first?"

I take a deep breath and frown. "How does your side not know this?"

"Back up a minute. Why does Margery want to close the Gates of Hell, when it's her job to open them?"

"She says she prefers her life on Earth the way it is."

"Bullshit. There's something more to this." Trisha looks down in thought and grinds the toe of her high heel into the pavement. Her breath's audible with a hint of irritation. Eventually she says, "I've got to get this information back to the angels."

"Wait. What about me? Does this get me out of trouble?" I want to ask her about Nina too but this isn't the time to press my luck.

"Not even close." Again she pokes my chest with her sharp nail. "You're my bitch until I say otherwise."

Great. More opportunities to fuck up.

Trisha looks up at the sky, places fingers under her tongue, and whistles. "First thing you'll do is deliver a package to Margery."

A white warrior descends carrying something the size of a bowling ball that's wrapped in clear plastic. It hisses at me and drops the package into Trisha's hands. Then it flies away.

She throws the package to me.

For once, I make the catch. It's Vern's head, bloody at the neck with his tongue hanging out. "What the fuck?" I let him drop to the pavement and rub my hands on my shirt.

"Had to be done. He's of no use to us and he's become too much of a troublemaker." She nudges Vern's nose with the spike on her heel. "In case you don't already know, beheading is the only way to kill one of you drivers. Be careful not to lose yours. You don't want the afterlife of a courier."

I pick up Vern and hold him at arm's length. "You want me to deliver Vern's head to Margery?" The thought of it makes my heart race.

"It'll send a pretty good message, don't you think?" She raises an eyebrow and bounces.

"As long as she doesn't kill the messenger." At the very least, she'll light an entire pack of cigarettes and throw them at the nearest mark, me.

She pulls me away from the driver side door. "Are the keys in the truck?"

"Yeah. Why?"

"I'm taking the kids." She climbs into the cab, and before she closes the door says, "I'll be in touch." Then she's gone.

No surprise, the Mustang she was standing beside earlier is gone too. I look at Vern's decomposing face and shrug. "Guess we're walking."

Chapter 19

A southern Colorado highway this late on a hot morning is like being on a Clint Eastwood Spaghetti Western. The dry terrain suffocates with the mix of scrub grass, dirt and asphalt. Straight ahead, heat haze rises from a wet mirage. Not even a gust from a passing semi truck provides relief from the sun beating down on our heads.

I pause to wipe my brow on the arm that carries Vern's head. This close to the poor bastard's face, it's obvious he'll be nothing but melty gelatin and skull by the time we reach Trinidad. Still prettier than what Margery will do to me when she finds out Vern's dead and Trisha's got all the kids for the sacrifice.

I look into Vern's open eyes. "How you doing, buddy?"

Air escapes his mouth and leaves a circle of steam on the plastic that covers his face. A mix of cigar breath and rotting flesh seeps through the bag. He's ripening faster than anticipated. I cringe and avert my attention to oncoming traffic.

Three vehicles, including a red OTG van, approach from the north. I jump and wave my arms, Vern's head flaps around. Any passerby who could make out this hitchhiker's luggage would be horrified. Good thing no cops are approaching.

The van passes but pulls over twenty or so yards down the road. "Yes," I whisper and run to catch up.

Nina's behind the wheel. "Bear, why you walking? Where's your van?"

Intent on freaking her out, I shove Vern's head into the vehicle first.

"Here, hold this for me."

She recoils and plasters her body against the driver side door. With her hands against her cheeks, she screams.

I snap him back. Teasing her was a stupid move, but that doesn't stop me from laughing. "If you're going to work for Margery, you're going to have to toughen up." I put Vern on the floor, climb into the seat, and tell her, "Drive."

Nina pulls onto the highway without checking traffic. A passing car nearly sideswipes us.

"What the hell are you doing?" I grip the dashboard with both hands.

She veers left and whimpers, "Are you going to hurt me?" A horn blares as another car passes.

"Watch the road!" I reach to steer the van back into our lane. Her driving is more dangerous than God's and Satan's armies combined. "I didn't cut off his head, okay?"

"Who did?"

"Never mind, just drive." If I tell her about Trisha, white warriors, and the Gates of Hell, she won't believe me anyway.

After a few miles of silence, Nina says, "What happened to you, Barry? You used to be so nice. Now you're punching old ladies and carrying the severed head of God knows who." A tear trails down her cheek.

"His name's Vern, and he has nothing to do with God." I suck in air, ready to laugh, but stop myself.

"Bear, the guy's dead."

"If you knew Vern, you'd know the world's a better place without him." And ranchers everywhere should breathe a sigh of relief.

"See what I mean? So callous."

Something hits the roof with a thud. The van rocks. I check above for white warriors. Nothing but clear blue sky. Then a white sphere, like the one that hit my truck, bounces off the windshield but doesn't break. Why would it? Margery put protection on this vehicle.

The steering wheel shakes from the force. Nina throws up her hands and starts to cry. "I can't…I can't do this again."

I grab the wheel and turn left, but not before the van's off the road, bouncing over the rough ground, and headed toward a barbed-wire fence. "Brake! Hit the brake!"

She's frozen from fright. I have to push her legs out of the way with my foot and press hard on the brake pedal. When we stop short of a fencepost, I'm half in the driver's seat with Nina beside me, scrunched against the door. "What the hell's wrong with you?" I ask.

Besides streaming tears, she chatters something mixed with giant birds and panic attacks. "I'll quit," she says. "That's what I'll do. Quit when we get to Trinidad."

She reminds me of my first day, and I feel bad about yelling at her. But I still want to shake her back to reality. Instead, I get in her face. "Trust me, quitting is not an option. You can do this. You have to."

Nina stops crying and looks into my eyes.

"Put the van in park," I tell her.

She's still staring at me weird, in a way women hardly ever look at me.

"Are you going to park it or what?" I move in closer.

She leans in too but not for the gearshift. Our lips meet and time stands still. Only the moment is stiff and not at all how I'd imagined a first kiss with Nina would be. I tense and pull away, then put the van in park.

"What's the matter?" She frowns.

"Why'd you do that?"

"Do what?" Her voice cracks.

"Why'd you kiss me?" What I really want to know is what changed her mind. All she's ever wanted is a friend who does stuff for her. Why, all of the sudden, am I good enough to kiss? Or is it that now I'm the kissable bad boy she likes?

"What's with you?" she says. "You kissed me too."

"Well, we shouldn't do it again." *Did I just say that?* My stomach drops with instant regret.

Nina frowns and pushes on my chest. "You're an ass."

I fall back into my seat and reach for the door handle. "Get out," I tell her.

"You're not leaving me here for kissing you, are you?"

"Of course not. We need to swap seats. I'm driving."

Chapter 20

NINA THRASHES around in the passenger seat, trying to keep her feet away from Vern's head. She points downward. "Is there some place else you can put *that*?" Other than periodic sighs, it's the first thing she's said since we got back on the highway an hour ago.

She's creeped out, and the foul odor Vern emits—a cross between cigar smoke and roadkill—is becoming more of a problem. I veer into the median and park. "Hand me the head," I say and hold out my hand.

"I'm not touching it." She scrunches her face in disgust.

"C'mon. It's wrapped up."

"No way."

"Fine." I yank the bag up from the floorboard. The plastic grazes her leg.

"You did that on purpose." She brushes away Vern's cooties.

I shake my head, get out, and pull the master key for the vans out of my pocket. I kept one after loading vans last night.

Weird. The door handle is longer and slimmer than the standard one from yesterday. And the key is larger than the hole. I jiggle the handle but it won't open. *What are you up to, Margery?* You changed the door locks and sent Vern and I out in unprotected vans. Why all the changes, and more so, why all the mistakes?

I lift the bag and say to Vern, "Looks like we'll both have to put up with Nina's whining for another hour. Maybe I'll play loud music you'll both hate."

Vern's mouth opens wider and he burps.

I turn up my nose. "I'm not sure if you're nastier alive or dead."

"Barry!" Nina calls out from the passenger side window. "Barry! Margery's asking for you."

I roll my eyes. This is not a conversation I want to have until we get to Trinidad. Then again, delivering bad news this far from her cursed cigarettes could be a good thing.

Back in the van, I don't give Nina a choice. I drop Vern in her lap. "Here. I don't have the right key for the back."

Nina jumps and knocks the package to the floor. "Jerk." She sticks her tongue out. "Margery, you should see what he's doing."

Margery snaps back with an echo, "Shut up, Girlie."

Nina looks around the cab, as if trying to figure out where Margery's voice is coming from.

I say sarcastically, "What do you want…Marge?"

"I don't think I like your tone…Honey."

"Hey, my tone is your fault. You sent Vern and me out in unprotected trucks."

"Oh, that." Margery hacks out a laugh, then her voice turns angry. "Nina said she picked you up south of Colorado Springs. What happened to your truck?"

"Angel's apprentice mean anything to you?"

A long draw on a cigarette resonates, followed by a forced exhale for several seconds. Finally, she says, "Where's Vern?"

I'm afraid to answer, but Nina has no such qualms and eagerly jumps. "He's dead. We have his head."

Margery growls so loud the van rocks. "You have thirty minutes to get to the warehouse." A stream of hot air fills the cab, and we have to open the windows.

"We're an hour away," I complain, but she's gone.

I turn my head to Nina. She's got her feet up on the seat, hugging her legs.

Her face scrunches as she says, "This may sound weird, but I think

Vern bit my ankle."

"No. Not weird." I pull onto the highway and gun the engine. "There are a few things I should tell you about Margery's operation before we get to Trinidad."

Chapter 21

We arrive at the warehouse in thirty-five minutes. Five minutes late. Who knows what our punishment will be. So I warn Nina to stay clear of Margery's cigarette.

Inside the garage, I swerve through an obstacle course of engine parts thrown all over the floor. Off to the side, in her seven-foot tall demon form, Margery's fiery hair blazes a few feet higher than the top of her skull. She pokes at Oscar's chest with her bulbous finger. Somehow he manages to stand proud and take it, pissing her off even more.

Nina leans over me to see out the driver's side window. "What the heck is that?" Her body shivers and she digs her fingers into my arm.

"That's Margery having a temper tantrum." My heart pounds at the prospect of another run-in with Margery. I bury my nose in Nina's hair and inhale the smell of her strawberry shampoo, calming my nerves.

Nina sits up and our heads knock. She glares at me like I'm some sort of freaky creep. Then, with a half giggle, she says, Everything you just told me is true. I mean, seriously, the Gates of Hell and child sacrifices are things that only happen in fiction."

"Had to see it to believe it, huh?" Sure Margery was listening in. I start to regret telling Nina so much, especially about the child sacrifice.

I turn off the engine, fall back in my seat, and let out all my breath. "Do me a favor, when we get out, keep your mouth shut and stay behind me."

After we exit the van, I push my door closed, so as not to draw attention. Nina, on the other hand, slams hers. My shoulders curl forward and I close my eyes for half a breath.

Margery taps her size-twenty-five foot and deflates back to a shriveled old lady, although I doubt that means she's happy to see us. "You two wait for me at my desk." She flips two cigarettes our direction and both hit *me* like lightning bolts.

I grab Nina's hand and pull her out of the garage.

"Why did she do that?" Nina whispers.

"Shut up or we'll end up like Vern." I squeeze her hand to let her know I'm serious.

As Nina and I round the corner into the lobby, Margery's already at her desk with her feet up, puffing on a cigar. "I don't know how Vern smoked these things," she says.

I wince, wondering how much more pain she could pack into a stogie than a cigarette.

"I'm sorry about Vern," Nina says, then leans in to me and whispers, "How did she beat us here?"

"Shut up, Girlie." Margery clasps the cigar in her fist. When she releases her grip, a lit cigarette is in its place.

Nina's lip quivers. "Why does everyone keep telling me to shut up?"

After a long sigh, I guide Nina to a chair and invite her to sit down. "Seriously, shut up."

Nina's whole body shakes and tears streams down her onto cheeks. "I know I'm supposed to be quiet, but I feel really dizzy." She barely finishes her sentence when she leans to one side and falls to the floor, landing on her face.

I choke to stifle a laugh.

"Ah, you are evil." By the look on Margery's face, she's pleased by my reaction.

I clear my throat and rush to lift Nina off the floor. She's unsteady. Her blonde hair hangs over her eyes as she fumbles for the seat. My lips brush against her ear as I whisper, "Sorry."

"Tell her to knock off the drama," Margery says, "or she'll end up like Vern."

I snap back, "Give her a chance to get used to it all." Then I wait for retaliation for spilling my guts about the kids. It doesn't come, at least not yet.

"No time." Margery turns her attention to Nina. "Get used to this face, Girlie. Now that Barry told you all about our plan to close the Gates of Hell, consider yourself promoted to my personal assistant so I can keep an eye on you."

Absolute panic replaces the weepy look on Nina's face.

I hold her shoulder in case she passes out again. "She won't last five minutes with you," I say and realize I'm scaring her more. "Let her stay with me."

"Not a chance. Besides, I've got plenty of work for her to do." Margery turns up an evil grin. "How are your filing skills, Girlie? I'm a few hundred years behind on filing contracts.

Still frozen in place, Nina doesn't answer.

I nudge her.

Margery leans in. "Or maybe I should send you out to the Bellow's Ranch to work for the demons. They'd be more than happy to keep a close eye on a pretty thing like you. And a few razor sharp claws too."

Nina's quick to respond this time. "I can file."

Oscar interrupts, both of his eye sockets are black and blue up to his eyebrows. There's no change in his demeanor. It's as if a beating is another part of an average day. "Cleaning the vans is not in my job description." He holds up Vern's unwrapped head by the tuft of his bad comb-over.

"Gimme that," Margery holds out her hands. Then she mumbles something that ends in, "…that bitch Trisha."

Oscar throws what's left of Vern over Nina's head. A chunk of flesh falls on her lap. She jumps up out of my arms and tip toes backward, "Get it off! Get it off me!" The chunk slides to the floor leaving a bloody streak on her skirt.

I gag.

With one hand on her hip, Margery raises her voice. "Shut her up."

I reach for Nina and pull her back to her seat. She needs to calm down, but I don't know what to do other than hold her hand.

Margery sets Vern upright on the table and slaps his cheek. "There might be a minute's worth of life left in him. Enough to ask him a few questions."

Vern has shown minor signs of life, but how can he talk with a squished face on one side and his lower lip puffed out? I lean in to get a better look and swallow hard. What might he say? Has he overheard anything that might get me in trouble?

Margery pounds her fist on top of Vern's head. Bloody goo oozes out from under his neck.

By now I'm expecting Nina to pass out again. Instead, she's frozen in place, her lip curled. I rub her back.

"Wake up," Margery says, but there's no response. After a second, his eyes pop open. Margery leans in and yells in his face. "Welcome back, dumbass!"

Vern spits coagulated blood. It splatters across Margery's face and clothes. "What happened?" he asks.

"For starters, look down and tell me what you see." Margery wipes her face with the back of her hand. "Someone, get me a wet towel." She juts her head at Nina and purses her lips.

Sending Nina to a room with a toilet seems like a good idea. I nudge her with my elbow and she runs from the room.

"My body." Vern gurgles. "Bitch cut off my head."

"Bingo," Margery says, "and you have about thirty seconds to answer my questions, so think with that rotting brain before you speak."

One of Vern's eyes widens, the other appearing paralyzed. "There are no animals in Hell."

"We don't have time to discuss your vices." Margery rolls her eyes and flicks his nose.

I hope Hell's management reserved a special corner for the bastard.

Margery leans near Vern's face. "Did you tell Trisha the sacrifice is tonight?"

My eyes widen. Tonight? If Trisha took the kids, how can the plan go down tonight? This has something to do with her not putting a hex on the trucks, but what?

When Vern's eyes close, Margery whacks him a couple more times. "Well, did you tell her about tonight or what?"

Bloody bubbles blow from Vern's mouth and his eyes shut.

"Damn it! He's gone to Hell's refugee camp." She picks up Vern's head and throws it across the room. "Where's that girl with my towels?" she yells, holding out both hands.

"I'm sure she's on her way back," I say. "Give her a minute."

"She's used up enough minutes. The only thing she's good for—"

I hold up my hands and back away. "I'll get your towels."

Chapter 22

Nina stares into the bathroom mirror, wiping tears from her cheeks with a long piece of toilet paper that's still attached to a roll in a stall. I've never seen her hair so messy. She cries harder when she sees me.

"Don't let Margery get to you. It only encourages her." I turn on the hot water and pull a half dozen paper towels from the dispenser. "Here. Wet these and take them to her."

"You do it. She'll just find something else wrong with me."

"It'll be worse if you don't bring them to her." I wet the towels and squeeze out the excess water. "She paralyzed me and made me piss my pants on my first day."

Nina smiles and takes the wad of wet paper towels from me. "Tell me this isn't happening."

"Wish I could, but I'd be lying." I pull some dry towels from the dispenser. "Here. Take these too. She'll probably want to dry off."

"I'm so glad you're here with me." She stretches up on her toes and kisses the air in the direction of my cheek. Then she runs from the bathroom.

My cheek tingles as if her lips had touched my skin. I lean over the sink and look at myself in the mirror. When I catch sight of the tired look on my face, fear replaces the pleasant feeling brought on by Nina. I wonder what I'll look like if I'm unable to help Trisha, and Margery's able to follow through with the sacrifice.

A tapping to my left interrupts my worried thoughts. I turn my head. Something, probably a rock, hits the window with the next tap. I walk over and peek outside. About forty feet away from the building, Trisha is crouched under a bush. She waves at me to join her.

The window's unlocked and slides to the side easily enough on the metal track. Luckily, there's no screen. I lean my head out and look for Oscar or anyone else. No one's there, so I hop up on the sill and jump out the window. The gravel crunches under my feet.

From inside a cluster of sticker bushes, Trisha says, "Get in here."

"How? With the thorns?"

"Would you rather get a few scratches or be caught with me?"

Thorns puncture my skin as I crawl inside. I jerk around to avoid the painful pricks but end up with more scratches. Droplets of blood form on my arms but quickly heal thanks to immortal life.

"Hold still," Trisha says.

"It hurts."

"A few scratches are the least of your worries right now. There were no kids in those trucks."

"What?" I play dumb even though we both know what Margery's capable of doing.

"You heard me," she says, her stare more barbed than the thorns. "Where are the kids?"

"How should I know? Margery said the plan's going down tonight, but I assumed your taking the kids changed that. If you don't have them—" I stop short when I remember the different door lock on the back of Nina's van. "Damn her. Vern and I were in unprotected vans because we were decoys," I tell Trisha. "She must have put the kids in the vans."

"The vans?"

"Yeah. I have a master key for the back doors on the vans, only Margery changed the locks."

"You're telling me we fell for one of the oldest tricks in the book." Trisha purses her lips and takes a deep breath. "Back up. Did you say the sacrifice is tonight?"

I nod my head.

"What else haven't you told me?"

"Nothing. I swear. I just found out."

"This is not turning out like I'd hoped. We have to stop her from hurting those kids, not to mention make sure the Gates of Hell don't open." Trisha closes her eyes. After a short pause, she snaps her fingers. "I've got it. Find a breach in the shield around the Bellows' Ranch, a way for the white warriors and I to get in and save the kids."

"Anything else you want me to do, like rob the Denver Mint? That would be easier."

"You joke, but it's the only way."

"Exactly how do you expect me to find something like that?"

"You want out of your contract?" she asks.

"Of course I do."

"Then you'll get us on the ranch."

"And if Margery catches me snooping around, are you going to save my head?"

Trisha laughs.

I sigh as all my regrets over the last few days flood my thoughts. "Why can't you make me one of those white warriors?" I say. "Let me fight with them."

"Why would I turn you when you're the only one who can help me get on the ranch?" she says. "Have faith and you'll figure it out. When you do, come back here to the bush and call out my name."

Chapter 23

AFTER CLIMBING back through the window, I exit the women's restroom at the same time Oscar comes out of the men's room. We both jerk to a stop and stare. I blink first. The guy scares the crap out of me.

"At least you know your place," he says with his usual scowl.

"You do have a sense of humor." I scan up and down the hallway. "Where's Margery?"

"Meeting in Hell."

"Again?"

Oscar turns away and limps in the direction of the garage, his braid swinging behind him.

"Hey, Oscar." I shuffle to catch up. "You been out at the Bellow's Ranch?"

"Many times. Why?"

"I might have to go out there tonight. Wondering what to expect."

"Stay clear of demons and hellhounds and you will be fine."

"Demons and hellhounds?" I keep after him, even though I'm afraid of his answer.

"Mean bastards. Sometimes Margery sends drivers out there just to get rid of them," he says. "Not that she wants to get rid of you."

I pause, swallow hard, and think how Margery's been threatening to send Nina to the ranch.

Oscar turns into the garage and I follow. "How do you get on and off the ranch?" I ask.

"Drive."

"Is that the only way?"

Oscar turns and glares at me. "Why you asking so many questions?"

"If I go out there tonight, I mean, what if something happens? I don't want any trouble."

"There are other ways." Oscar reaches into a tool chest, pulls out a hammer, and holds it up like he might use it on my head. "No more questions."

Chapter 24

W ITH MARGERY off in Hell and all the other drivers on their way back to Denver, the lobby's quiet. As usual, papers are scattered across the top of her table. Demons have no sense of organization, but who am I to point fingers?

Other ways? What other way could there be besides driving onto the ranch? *Airplane? Helicopter?* Not a chance I'll get my hands on either, not to mention I lack the skills to operate them. Besides, it's a stupid idea, considering the white warriors can fly.

Airshafts? Vern described the hellhole as being a part of the coal mine ventilation system. If Trisha and her warriors could access the airshafts… But how do I find the specs for a mid-twentieth-century coal mine without also heading to the county building?

As much paper as Margery keeps, there have to be records or maps of the underground around here somewhere. Then again, if white warriors can't get at the vans, how would they get underground near the hellhole?

The door off the lobby where Margery comes and goes opens. Nina pokes her head out. "What you doing, Bear?" She's got this forced grin she gets when she's about to ask for a favor.

"Looking for something." I shuffle through a stack of what appears to be the new drivers' contracts. Damn, nothing of any use. I turn to Nina and ask, "What are you doing?"

"Filing." Nina rolls her eyes. "What are you looking for?"

I probably shouldn't tell her. I've already gotten her in enough trouble. "Nothing important."

"There's a lot more paperwork in here if you can't find what you're looking for," she says. "More paper than a world full of trees could provide."

I run my hands through my hair, squeeze my head, and look at her with a frown.

She waves me over. "C'mon, I'll show you."

Inside the room, we weave through a maze of stacked papers. Some of the piles tower out of reach. Margery wasn't kidding about the backlog of filing. Overhead, naked lightbulbs float in a black void. There's no telling the size of the room because there are no walls in sight. This could take Nina an eternity to sort through.

A single metal file cabinet, black as night, sits in the midst of it all. It's old and dented, as if it's been here since the beginning of time.

"Get this," Nina says. "I have to file all this paperwork into that one file cabinet, and it's already full."

Hell could use a database, but data entry for this mess would take Nina two eternities.

I pull out the second drawer from the top and examine the contents. A typical alphabetic filing system, but she's right, it's completely packed with overstuffed manila folders. Getting a single piece of paper in the thing will be a struggle. I'm afraid to ask. "Did she give you a deadline?"

"No. I think she put me in here to get me out of her crazy hair." Nina's voice wavers. "I have no idea where to start."

Knowing that Nina fears anything new, I take over like I always do. "Give me one of those contracts."

She hands me a two-inch stack of legal-sized paper with the name "Abe Templeton" on it.

I close the second drawer and open the bottom one, labeled S-Z on the outside for files at the end of the alphabet. There's a tab for the letter 'T' up front, and no surprise, there's already a file for Abe. I manage to slip my index finger into the folder.

"Good luck getting it in there," Nina says.

"You forget that nothing's as it seems around here." I slowly lower the contract toward the drawer. One at a time, every last page is sucked into the file cabinet as if the thing is part vacuum. I pull my hand back before it pulls me in too.

Nina claps and hops. "You're a magician."

"Easy enough to put them in," I say, "but for my next trick, I'll pull out my contract." Could it be that easy? Just remove my own contract and rip it up. I finger the tabs through to the letter 'F' for 'Frost.' Nothing.

"Bear, you're forgetting she's a hundred years behind on filing. Our contracts could be anywhere."

"Damn." I slam the door shut.

Nina pushes me out of the way. "What were you looking for on Margery's desk? Maybe we can find it in the cabinet."

I shake my head. "You're better off not knowing."

"You're always taking care of me," she says. "It's my turn to help you."

I hesitate. It's bad enough imagining what Margery will do if she finds me snooping around for specs to the airshafts. "Are you prepared to have your fingernails pulled off if Margery finds out you're helping me? Because I'd never forgive myself if that bitch hurt you."

"If you're doing anything that will help us out of our contracts, she can have my toenails too." She moves in closer and bats her green eyes at me. "Let me help you."

I sigh and give in to her pleading. "I'm looking for maps of a ventilation system into an abandoned coal mine where the Gates of Hell are about to open."

She pauses with an inquisitive frown. "Well, we could look under maps or airshafts or, maybe, tunnels." We look, but there's nothing.

"Let me check for a Bellows' Ranch file," I tell her and cross my fingers. When I pull out the drawer that includes a 'B' it's there, taking up the entire drawer, as if the cabinet knew what I wanted. I flip through the file and search for anything that looks like a map, but nothing even close to a drawing exists. It's all invoices for payment in tons of silver, paid out to the owner of the ranch, Charles K. Bellows.

"Barry." Nina's voice is muffled and distant.

I look around, but she's gone. Oh hell, what's she into now? My heart skips as I rush farther into the room.

"Barry!" she calls out again. "Hurry!"

"Hang on!" I jog into the maze of stacked paper, expecting to have to save her cute ass yet again.

She's standing in front of rolled-up blueprints, stacked up into a dark void. They look like a honeycomb. Nina holds one up that's partially unrolled. There's a giant grin on her face. "I found it. I can't believe I found it!"

I take it from her and spread the roll of three maps across the floor: one of the warehouse, one of the ranch, and one of a tunnel system connecting the two. Each tunnel connects into a vertical airshaft. At the center of it all, the widest opening to the surface must be the hellhole. There's writing at each junction that I'm pretty sure is Latin, but translating it is way outside my skill-set. Hopefully Trisha will understand what it says. One would assume Latin would be a prerequisite for angels' apprentices.

I turn to Nina. "This is better than I'd hoped for." I'm just about to stand back up and kiss her when the door opens.

Margery calls out, "Hey! Girlie! Where are you? I said no breaks."

We both jump when the door slams, our eyes wide and honed in on each other. Nina holds her finger up to her lips to shush me. "Coming!" Then she whispers to me, "I'll get rid of her."

I shake my head and reach to grab her wrist, but she slips away.

"I'm sorry," Nina says to Margery. "I'm just so tired, I must have nodded off."

"You worthless little—" Margery's voice deepens.

"Really, Marge," Nina says. "You sound like my mother."

My stomach drops. Did Nina just have the guts to say that?

"You want a mother figure? Come here. I'll give you a mother figure." By Margery's tone, she's already morphed seven feet tall with flames shooting out of her scaly head.

Nina screams.

I take a few steps forward. I want to save her, but a voice in my head tells me to get the maps to Trisha first.

Chapter 25

ITAKE A shortcut through the garage on my way to the bushes where I last met up with Trisha. In a rush to get around the corner, I ricochet off Oscar and crash into a wall. The blueprints flies up into the air.

Oscar catches the tube in one hand and momentarily holds it above his head. "Why you in such a hurry?"

"Fresh air." I take back the map but not without a tug of war that crinkles the maps at the center. Before he can ask me another question, I'm safely out the door, diving into a thorn bush.

"Trisha," I whisper, "I've got something for you."

Trisha appears out of thin air. She's so close to my face I notice she smells like roses. Her hair is all messy, like the first time we met. Only now I know it's not a walk of shame she's been on; she's been out fighting the forces of evil. "That was fast. This better be good."

I jerk my neck back and hold out the blueprints. "Maps of the warehouse, ranch, and the tunnels connecting them."

She snatches the tube out of my hand, her eyes boring into me. "I already know about the tunnels, and I can't access them."

"At least take a look. Maybe there's something you don't know about in the text." I reach for the map. My fingers fumble to help her open it. "Nina found them. That counts toward getting her out of her contract, right?"

She ignores me and studies the map, the look on her face unreadable.

"What do you think?" I reach in and nervously point at the text.

"Can you use it?"

"Use it? Barry, you have no idea how valuable a find this is."

I let out a long sigh of relief. Finally, I did something right. Again I ask, "Is this enough to get us out of our contracts?"

"Go back inside." Trisha rolls the blueprints back up. She taps me across the cheek with the tube. "Don't let on about this, and do whatever Margery tells you to do."

Damn, I'm still her bitch. "What if I do something against one of those Ten Commandments your side is always preaching about? Will God hold it against me?"

"Don't worry about that. It's more important to make it look like you're on Margery's side, or she might get wise to us," she says. "Now go. If I need you, I'll find you." Trisha disappears with the maps.

Something's not right about this wannabe angel telling me to be bad, but I don't have time to worry about it. I have to save Nina.

Chapter 26

I WALK BACK into the garage and turn my head to avoid Oscar's glare.

"How is the air?" he asks.

I keep moving forward and walk faster, Nina's wellbeing is my only concern.

"Stop," Oscar calls out.

I turn with a pinched expression. "What?"

"We must retrieve something for Margery." He waves a fist-sized gray sack by the drawstring, then throws it up into the air.

I catch it. The bag clinks in my hand. From the way it feels in my fingers, it could be coins. "Will this take long? I've got to get back to Nina?"

"No need. This is for your girlfriend. She tried to run away while you were outside. Margery does not enjoy chasing down drivers." He steps closer and juts out his chin. "Margery is sending us to retrieve her punishment."

Great. I don't want any part of disciplining Nina. The possibility of what we're going after terrifies me. It's also unnecessary considering Margery can get anyone to do anything with one puff of her cigarette.

Oscar leads the way outside through the garage door. We turn right, around the east side of the building.

Grasshoppers hop around us as we approach a patio. Tall brown grass and wild sunflowers grow between cracks in the cement. Off to one side sits a picnic table with a bench on its side. The air smells like rotting trash even though no one would ever come back here to eat.

With cigarette and cigar butts scattered everywhere, I can almost see Margery and Vern here, smoking and plotting better ways to torture the new drivers.

We stop in front of two vintage soda machines lined against the exterior wall of the warehouse. "Put the coins in the blue machine," Oscar tells me.

I untie the sack and find it filled with gold coins stamped with a picture of an old man riding a crocodile. "Dang, that's some expensive soda. What kind of money is this?"

He crosses his arms. "It is not money. It is an offering."

I approach the coin slot. "Put all of them in?"

Oscar nods his head.

At first I step forward and pull a coin out of the bag but stop short. Whatever punishment the machine serves up from Hell, why make me get it?

I turn to Oscar and tell him, "No. Not until you tell me what we're doing."

Oscar gnashes his teeth and rushes at me. He takes hold of the collar on my t-shirt and twists the fabric until it restricts my airway. Then, just as quickly, he lets me go.

After taking a few steps back, I clutch my neck and cough. "What the hell?" My nostrils flare as I adjust my t-shirt back in place.

A vein throbs on his forehead. "Stop wasting my time."

I think how Trisha told me to blindly play along, but this can't be good. And before working for Margery, doing what I'm told has never been my strong suit. "I'm not doing this without an explanation."

Oscar crosses his arms and returns to his usual dull tone. "The coins are an offering to Agares, head of Eastern Hell. He is the old man pictured on the coin. If he accepts, which he will, he will dispatch the essence of one of the demons in his charge. It will dispense there." Oscar points at the slot where a can of soda would normally fall. "Margery means to possess Nina with the essence and use it to control her."

My eyes bulge and my chest tightens. I yell at him, "Like Linda Blare in the Exorcist? And Margery expects me to go along with this?"

Oscar unzips his coveralls down to his belly button. He points at a bumpy baseball-sized scar below his breastbone. "Insertion is quick, and I do not remember the pain."

One of my eyes reacts with a nervous twitch. "You've got a damn demon in you?" *That actually explains a lot.*

"No. It was removed because I behave. Nina will learn to behave too," he says. "Now insert the coins, or I will tell Margery you have chosen to send Nina to the ranch. You have chosen to never see her again. You have chosen to send her where no one will ever see her again."

"Those are your words, not mine," I say with a raised voice, then calm myself to add, "Wait a minute. What do you mean, Nina will learn?"

"I was once rebellious like your girlfriend. Margery put the same type of demon in me. I no longer had the will or want to leave."

"She put the same demon in you?"

"You never listen. Same type, not same demon." He takes a deep breath, moves in, and pushes the back of my shoulder. "Put in the coins...*now.*"

I stand firm, balance the offering on my palm, and mumble, "This is insane, buying demons from a freakin' vending machine."

Oscar swipes the bag from my hand and pushes me out of the way. He inserts the coins in the slot, then moves in and presses a sequence of flavors: cola, orange, lemon-lime, orange, orange, cola, lemon-lime, as if entering a code. With his hand held up, he says, "Get ready. It will slither out like an anaconda ready for a meal. I will grab the end that comes out first. You grab the other end before it comes all the way through. Hold it away from your torso or it will try to enter your body." He hits orange one last time.

The cooling system kicks on and I shiver. The motor purrs at first, then amplifies into a screeching whine. I jump when something drops with a clunk, the same sound you hear when a soda can drops, but louder. When the motor shuts off, I notice the power cord for the vending machine is not plugged into an outlet. I doubt that means it's battery operated.

"Come closer," Oscar says.

A black curvy tip—a cross between a bird's beak and a rattlesnake's tail—edges its way out. The thing is connected to a jagged diamond-shaped head. It twitches, as if sniffing at the air.

Oscar grabs it. "I said, come closer."

The thought of touching the thing makes me shiver, and having it in my hands means it's a step closer to possessing Nina. I don't want to be a part of this. I can't be a part of this.

Oscar holds on tightly as it bucks against the inside of the machine. "Grab it or I will let it bore up your asshole."

"All right, all right." I drag my feet to the opening and lean in.

Oscar tugs it away from the machine. What comes into view appears to be a spine or backbone, but more ornate than a human's or animal's. It reminds me of spiky dinosaur bones.

I take it in my hands. The bristly surface pricks at my palms. I keep it at arms length while it bends and veers toward my torso. The longer we hold it, the more wildly it bucks. I don't dare let go of the thing out of fear it will get loose and claim me.

"Hurry," Oscar says as we turn to enter the garage.

I take rapid breaths at the thought of the thing burrowing into Nina. Playing a role in a human possession qualifies as stupid. My head spins and my body freezes in place. "I can't do this."

Oscar pauses in mid stride. He turns back to me. "You can and will, or you are responsible for worse things that will happen to your girlfriend."

"You keep saying that, but how is this better?"

"Trust me. Nina with a demon controlling her is better than Nina divided among demons."

"You mean that literally, don't you?"

Oscar nods, turns, and tugs the spine to prompt me to move.

I follow, but drag my feet.

Around the corner, into the breakroom, Nina's gagged and tied to a chair. She sees me, moans, and bounces in her chair.

All I can do is look away like a coward.

"Enough of your whining," Margery says. She's seven feet tall, black, and scaly. She extends a claw and snatches the spinal column away from us. It goes limp in the demon bitch's hand.

Damn her. "You're not doing this to control Nina, you're doing this to control me."

Margery turns to Oscar. "Sometimes I think the boy has half a brain." She pokes the tip of the spine at Nina's torso. The thing awakens and thrashes like a fish out of water, but with Margery's strength, she easily maintains control. "Does it turn you on, seeing your girlfriend so helpless?"

I growl and rush at Margery but run into the back of her scaly hand. She hurls me halfway across the room. I hit the wall and cough out all my breath.

Nina lets out a muffled scream and hops backward in her chair. She tips to one side and her head strikes the floor. She lays limp and still.

"Look at her. Out cold." Margery rolls her eyes. "I'll have to insert this demon without the satisfaction of hearing her scream."

Again, I jump to my feet and rush her. Again, she backhands me.

"Get him out of here," Margery says to Oscar. "Go ready the trucks for the trip to the ranch."

Oscar grabs the back of my t-shirt. My arms thrash as he drags me toward the door.

Chapter 27

Back in the garage, Oscar opens the back exit and pushes me out into the back alley. We both pause and look up into a sky filled with white warriors. At least a hundred hover over the warehouse and the surrounding grounds.

Oscar glares at me, and my guilty conscience says he suspects I'm the reason they're there. I grin and shrug. My only hope, that he didn't see me in the bushes with Trisha.

"Trucks are down there, at the loading docks with keys in the ignition." Oscar points down the alleyway. "Drive them up here to this door, then come back inside." He turns to leave.

"Wait. You sure Nina will be okay?"

"Time will tell with *that* demon in her." He laughs.

Oscar's happy? Oscar's never happy. "What do you mean, that demon?"

"I shorted the offering to Agares at the vending machines. Nina is possessed by a rebellious demon," he says. "It is doubtful the demon will behave any better than Nina."

I'm frozen in place at first, hunched over, mouth gaping. "What the…?" I shove Oscar then turn away, fighting the urge to plant my fist in his face, but it's not working. "Why?"

"I do not trust you," he says, "and I do not like you." Oscar turns and goes inside.

That's no reason to hurt Nina. "You need to tell Margery what you did." I rush after Oscar and reach for his shoulder.

He spins around and lands his fist in my eye.

I'm thrown off balance and shuffle backward out the door. I fall on my ass and skid across the gravel.

Oscar shakes his hand, then points at me. "Unless you want her headless, you will keep your mouth shut."

Chapter 28

AFTER MOVING the trucks, I'm back in the breakroom holding one ice pack against my bruised eye and another against my ribs. Thanks to my immortal healing, the pain is nearly gone from both Margery's and Oscar's hits.

Nina, or whatever controls her body now, sits across a table from me. She bounces her head like a bobble-head doll and scans the room with a sort of bizarre fascination. Her beautiful green irises have turned violet and the whites are bloodshot. Margery said it happens to humans more often than not from the shock of the insertion. The redness will fade; the violet is forever, a permanent reminder I did nothing to help her.

"Neeh…nuh." For a half hour now, she's been saying her name with short puffs of breath. Nothing else. She snaps her head and focuses my direction "Bah…ree?" She laughs, then repeats, "Bah…ree. Bah… ree. Bah…ree."

I rub my forehead and suck in a long breath. Too much more of this and I'll sell my soul a second time for earplugs.

Margery enters the room. The cigarette in her mouth bobs as she says, "Didn't take long for the demon to speak through her. Does it know Nina's name yet?"

"That's all it would say a minute ago, before it figured out my name." I roll my eyes.

"Good. Nina and the demon are communicating. They'll act more like one human in an hour or two," Margery says. "It's time to go. Drag her with you."

"No." Nina huffs and crosses her arms. "Stay…here."

Margery gets in her face and looks deep into her eyes. "I know you can both hear me. Cooperate, or you both go to the ranch."

"Go cluck…urself." Nina blinks rapidly, a smirk drawn across her face. In fact, she looks possessed.

"Great." Margery shakes her head. "I've replaced a moron with an idiot."

"Bod breath." Nina waves her hand over her nose.

With her cigarette pointed at Nina's head, Margery says, "Shut up."

The blinking stops and Nina's eyes pop, but the smirk is frozen in place. She holds up one hand to protect her face and the other flips Margery the bird. Her whole body is a contradiction of emotions, each struggling to dominate the other.

I grab the cherry tip of the cigarette and pull it away. "Stop!" Not my smartest move. The burn penetrates my fingers, followed by an electrical surge that has every hair on my body standing on end. Attach jumper cables to my ears and I could start a car. I throw the cigarette to the side. "*Damn.*"

Margery turns to leave. "You figure out how to bring the idiot and the moron outside to the trucks. We leave for the ranch in ten minutes."

It's a miracle she's giving up so easy.

I start to pace. *Ten minutes?* We're leaving already? Less than an hour ago I gave Trisha the maps. If she doesn't find a way in…

I look down at Nina while she takes off one of her strappy sandals. She looks at it with wonder. "Beautiful," she says. "Want more." She stands up and rushes for the door.

Great, a demon with a shoe fetish.

"No, no, you're coming with me." I chase after Nina, grab her hand, and pull her in close. "Do me a favor and follow Margery's orders, at least for now."

Nina spins around like a dancer and hits my chest. The force throws us both off balance and we stumble while she wraps her arms around my waist. She hugs me tightly. "You cute. Barry Gita's boyfriend."

This demon is out of control already. "Gita? Is that your demon name?" I chuckle. "Well, Gita, Barry don't do demons." I grab her shoulders and hold her at bay. It's obvious she'll do something stupid if I let her walk on her own, so I steer her out of the breakroom and down the dark hall.

Outside the garage, Margery calls to me, "Over here." She stands beside the two box trucks I moved earlier. "You're driving six-six-six-three." She throws a set of keys high up into the air. I lean away from Nina to catch them.

This is a repeat of this morning, when she sent us out in unprotected trucks. Hundreds of white warriors, soaring in the sky above doubles the jeopardy.

"Follow closely, especially on the ranch," Margery says, her eyes burning into me. "If you lose me and the hellhounds find you…"

"Yeah, yeah, I'll be hellhound kibble." I roll my eyes. "I'm more concerned about the truck I'm driving. Did you bother to protect it with one of your hexes? Or are the white warriors going to take me out five minutes into the drive?" I look upward and my stomach drops.

"The last thing I want is for the white warriors to get at the content of these trucks. Besides, would I let anything happen to my new favorite driver?" She winks.

I raise an eyebrow and stare at her, sure she's lying through her tobacco-stained teeth. At least she needs me to drive the kids safely to the airshaft. After that, there's nothing stopping her from feeding me to a hellhound.

My stomach churns again. This could be my demise. And Nina's end. Trisha's made no promises, and there's no reason for her to help us if she manages to save the kids.

Margery waves her cigarette in front of my face to break my stare. "Get in your truck."

I gag when I catch a whiff of her nicotine-stained fingers.

"You're coming with me, Girlie." Margery yanks Nina away from me. A look of terror in Nina's eyes tells Nina is also present.

"No," I say. "Let her come with me."

"So the two of you can run off? I don't think so. She's with me."

I nod my head at Nina and tell her, "It'll be okay. I'll be right behind you."

Nina stumbles after Margery and looks back at me. She holds up the sandal, still in her hand. "Want more," she says with tears in her eyes. "Want more."

"Later." I nod my head, worried she'll pester Margery to take her shoe shopping. Instead, she'd reach the ranch without feet. "I'll take you to every shoe store in Denver."

Chapter 29

I'M DRIVING behind Margery through a narrow gulch with red, jagged rock formations reaching twenty to thirty feet high on each side. Sunset orange clouds swirl in the sky above. Hundreds of white warriors hover like vultures, but it seems they can only descend so far, making them no threat.

I rub the back of my neck. Why are they intimidating us and not underground with Trisha? Is she having trouble finding a way in? Oh God, please tell me we're not screwed.

Margery exits the gulch into a clearing. I follow fifty feet behind her over a roadway overgrown with grass. I take my foot off the gas pedal and the space between us widens. Part of me wants to bail, make a u-turn, head back toward the warehouse. The knowing what Margery would do to Nina if I run keeps me on course.

Red taillights brighten on the back of Margery's truck. I follow her lead and brake but leave thirty feet between us. The right turn signal blinks on her truck. She lets up off the brake, slowly turns into the field, and vanishes into thin air.

I fall back in my seat and sigh. Margery said to follow her closely. Well, Margery, I did that. I punch the steering wheel with the heel of my hand. This reeks of another set up. Irritated, I let off the brake and gun the engine to where Margery stopped, then cut a hard right.

The sky turns pitch black as if someone's turned off a light switch. Ahead, the headlights illuminate a typical Colorado landscape: dry grass, sagebrush, and weathered rock formations.

I lean over the steering wheel and look up. No wonder Margery couldn't care less about the white warriors. They've all disappeared. Her warnings about hellhounds fill my head in their place. Although I've never seen one, common sense says anything coming after me out here ain't my friend.

I squint and scan the distance for taillights. Nothing. That doesn't stop me. I keep moving forward, the truck rocking side to side, scrambling the poor kids in the back of the truck. Maybe it's a good thing I'm lost. Maybe by some miracle, Margery will never find me and the kids will be safe.

A quarter mile later, continuing over a sea of half-buried boulders and sagebrush, white dots of light appear out of nowhere. I stop, assuming Margery has turned back to look for me, or that I've found the location of the hellhole.

There's a sudden movement to my left. I flinch and my head jerks to focus in on some sagebrush waving back and forth. I suck in air and hold my breath. What the hell is that?

A coyote chases a rabbit out of the bush and across the front of the truck.

I exhale and my lips rumble. Screw this. I'm getting the hell out of here. I turn the steering wheel away from the bush and gun the engine. The truck jumps forward; at the same time, another coyote scampers into the headlights. I blare the horn.

It halts and stares with red glowing eyes, then crouches and snarls.

I honk again.

It turns and runs, followed by three more of the bastards that come out of nowhere. They all rush into the darkness.

Good riddance. I hate coyotes. No better than a rat.

Then the thing that spooked them shows itself. Ten feet tall at its shoulders. Black leathery skin with cracks that radiate a fiery orange. There's no mistaking a hellhound even if you've never seen one. It runs like a gorilla on claws the size of my forearms and catches the slacker of the pack by the head. The beast chomps down on the coyote's neck, lifts the defenseless animal, and shakes it like a tug toy. The body tears away from its head and hurtles through the air. Where else would it land but on the windshield.

The carcass slides downward, leaving a smear of blood across the glass. I swallow hard and watch through red streaks as the hellhound gulps down the coyote's head. The monster turns, scans the terrain for the rest of its meal and zeros in on my truck. It roars a hundred times louder than a grizzly bear and bolts across the terrain, straight toward me.

In one fell swoop, the hellhound leaps onto the hood of the truck. One claw scrapes the hood and the other picks up the coyote. It gulps down the rest of the coyote like a great white shark.

The beast still looks hungry when it lowers its head and stares into the truck. A fog of hot breath and snot daub the glass.

My throat squeaks as I slowly slither down onto the floorboard. If only Margery's damned contract had given me bigger balls as well as immortal life.

There's a loud crash from above. Shards of glass rain down on my head. A claw scrapes against my leg, as if the hellhound's trying to dish up Barry flavored ice cream.

I kick upward at the bastard. My foot catches the gear shifter and the truck slips into drive. The creeping movement gives me the idea to run it over. I lean both hands onto the gas pedal until it hits the floor. The truck jerks forward, but the hellhound holds on. Its grip is too tight. I gas the truck and brake, gas it and brake until the truck hits something. I push down on the accelerator and the engine revs. The wheels spin. The truck's stuck.

I pause and rub my forehead, like that'll spark a lifesaving idea. That's when I notice it's quiet. Did the hellhound fall off the hood? Maybe, but I doubt he's given up.

I grope around the cab for something, anything that resembles a weapon. The tire iron under the passenger seat will have to do. I pull it out slowly, so as not to make any noise, then build up the courage to peek up over the dashboard.

Shit! A boulder blocks the left side of the truck, and the hellhound is lying on the ground, off to the right. It's not moving.

"Barry! Honey!" Margery pipes in over her demonic speaker system.

"Shh…" I say. Damn, her timing sucks.

The beast's head lifts, then drops.

"Where are you, Honey?"

"Margery, be quiet."

This time she yells, "Where are you?"

The hellhound lifts itself into a sitting position. It shakes and rubs its head. Smoke rises from its nose.

My own nostrils flare as I gasp for air. "Please. Margery. Shut Up."

"Why? What's going on?" She's even louder.

"Hellhound."

It jumps back onto all fours. Orange sparks fly off its back and snuff out in midair.

My grip tightens on the tire iron.

"Make noise!" Margery screams. "Make lots of noise, and turn the headlights on high beam. Bright light blurs their vision."

I reach for the horn, then freeze. Is she nuts? Draw more attention to myself? This is another one of her tricks.

"If it gets closer, throw something at it, anything and everything." She breaks to hack and cough. "Hold tight. I'm on my way."

The headlights are on high beam and that hasn't deterred it. Throw everything and anything at it? I look at the tire iron and then at the hellhound. I am *not* giving up my only weapon.

I position myself in the driver's seat, put the truck in reverse, and press the gas pedal. The engine revs as I pull back a few feet to clear the boulder.

The hellhound, on the other hand, scrapes a claw across the dirt.

It charges like a pissed off rhinoceros and plows headfirst into the headlight on the passenger side. A claw takes out the other headlight.

I spy veins of orange in the pitch blackness, my only clue to the beast's position. With one hand, I hold tight on the door handle and the tire iron with the other. When it jumps back on the hood and sticks its head through the windshield, I open the door and run for my life.

In less than twenty feet, the bastard jumps onto my back and forces me to the ground. I spit out a mouthful of dirt and wheeze as I try to inhale. It sniffs my head and growls. Or is that the sound of a truck engine? *Margery?*

The hellhound roars and exhales a hot breath that scorches the back of my head and all the way down my right arm. Its teeth penetrate the flesh at my elbow. I let out a high-pitched scream when my shoulder socket snaps and my skin tears as if I'm made of paper. Vomit rises in my throat as hellhound drool oozes over my hair and down my forehead. The hound takes my head into its mouth and I black out.

Chapter 30

"**H**EY, KID. Get up."

"Vern?" I recognize his voice, but I'm blind to his location.

"Get up," he repeats.

"It's so dark and cold." I grope at the air and add, "Where are we?"

"We're in the refugee camp." Vern tugs at my arm and guides me to my feet.

"What the hell am I doing here?"

"There's no time for conversation. We've got to move."

The darkness turns to blurry yet fiery oranges that lashes over me, leaving a burning sensation over my skin. Vern loses his grip on me and I'm forced backward. My head crashes to the ground first. Chatter echoes in my head, distinguishable as English, French, Cantonese and every other language on Earth. They speak their piece, but no one cares what the other has to say.

Their presence brushes over my body and lifts me. My skin crawls in a way that makes me want to scream. I reach outward and struggle to free myself. They toss me, to and fro, like a singer in a black metal band until I drop to the ground. Splitting pain explodes throughout my body.

The wind's knocked out of me. I struggle to catch my breath and fear they'll pick me up again. Instead, a heaviness overwhelms me and drives me onto my stomach. I give up and collapse. My only thought, stay still and maybe they'll leave.

By the time I've caught my breath, clunky footsteps replace the roar of the crowd. "Kid." Vern grabs my arm and helps me to my feet. "I suggest you get up before the next wave of refugees drop in on us."

"Man, am I glad to see you." Especially considering my vision has returned. I smile and pat both his shoulders.

He shoves me away and scans the area as if we're being watched. "Knock off the happy-to-see-you act. No one's glad to see anyone in the refugee camp."

"Yeah, about that, how did I end up here?"

"How'm I supposed to know?"

"Then tell me what that wave was," I say loudly and insert my fingers into my ears to rub away the buzzing. I feel a little stupid, as if I'm Vern's Nina.

"Consider that your unwelcome party. Those souls never showed an ounce of kindness to anyone during their lives. They flock together and fly around here in a tide of misery."

"What's up with the military uniform?" Vern's dressed to perfection in all black with sharp creases and brass buttons. Minus a swastika, he could be a Nazi colonel. Fitting, considering this place originated around the World Wars.

"I'm a guard. It's in our courier contract. Lose your head and spend eternity guardin' the overflow of damned souls." He crosses his arms and scans the area. "Just never figured I'd end up here."

"Why not?"

"For one thing, hundreds of years workin' for Marge. I helped start her operation in Trinidad. I deserve somethin' better than this. I mean, look at this place and take a big whiff of it."

I imagine he's missing his cigars, replaced with the smell of rotting trash and piss.

The horde appears to avoid us outside a three-foot bubble from where we stand. The forlorn figures wander aimlessly and as far as the eye can see. Some punch and kick at the air, some converse as if they're in a heated debate with themselves. Their moans are a constant electrical buzz in the air. It's like a rave where they took the good stuff out of the Ecstasy, and replaced it with angst and despair.

I shiver from the coldness in the air. Their torment is contagious, with symptoms of anger encasing my heart and panic welling in my gut. "I get it. This place sucks."

Vern glares at me.

"What are you guarding? I mean, no one seems in any hurry to go anywhere."

"If they don't want to be here, nothing keeps them in the camp but their own guilt. Most are just too stupid to know that," he says. "Us guards make sure they remain miserable, and that they don't get any silly ideas, like prayin'. Friggin' hope spreads like a bad case of the clap in a whorehouse. As soon as they start a group prayer, ten or twenty of 'em take off like rockets to Purgatory. And when we lose refugees"—Vern points at a massive troll-like demon sticking up twelve feet higher than the crowd—"those things beat on the nearest guard and we all feel it. Pain's amplified a hundred times worse here. Even more so than inside the walls of Hell."

"So all I have to do is pray to leave this place." My face perks up and I clap my hands together. "Our Father, Who art in Heaven…" I frown. Despite being dragged to church every Sunday as a kid by my mother—although no one would ever call me a good Catholic boy—I have forgotten The Lord's Prayer. Has to be the camp's energy, messing with my head. An excuse even my mother might buy.

It doesn't matter. Three souls in the crowd illuminate and light beams upward from their chests. They ascend on rays a hundred feet or so. Then, poof, they vanish. I, on the other hand, remain in the darkness, watching the troll demons close in on us. My shoulders slump.

Vern turns and walks away. "You're on your own."

"What am I supposed to do? Give up and put on a uniform?"

The demons back away, and the crowd returns to grounded chaos.

"Lucky for you, makin' an ass of yourself is excusable down here."

Vern shakes his head. "From what Margery says about you, I doubt they'd ever put you in a uniform. I doubt you're even dead."

I chase after Vern, unsure what he's talking about. "Wait, if that's true, how do I get back to Earth?"

He throws up his arms. "If I knew how to get out of this place, do you think I'd be standing here?"

"C'mon, Vern, there has to be a way out of here."

"What's the last thing you remember?"

I grab my neck. "Hellhound."

Vern nods his head and smiles. "How'd you manage to meet up with a hellhound?"

"How do you think? Margery led me right to it."

Vern stops and looks back at me. "You sure about that? I don't think Marge wants you dead." He walks away, and the refugees scurry to keep the three-foot distance as they do around the other guards.

"All I remember is tailing her down a dirt road one minute, and the next she disappeared into oblivion. I tried to follow her—"

"You took the wrong portal."

"Portal?"

"Not important, considerin' you ended up here." He averts his attention toward two of the trollish giants staring our directions. "We should leave this area. Looks like the demons figured out you don't belong here."

"What about getting me out of here?"

"Told ya. Don't know how."

Oscar's voice echoes in my head. "Barry."

I turn full circle in search of Oscar, although I know he isn't in the camp.

"Barry," he repeats, "if you can hear me, stay still."

"Kid," Vern says at the same time.

I feel a slap on my cheek but have no idea who did it because my vision's doubled. My senses are numb and confused. In an attempt to become lucid, I close my left eye and focus on Oscar, who's leaning over me, a bare light bulb above his head. When I close my right eye, Vern's staring at me. We're still in the refugee camp. Up above us, a bright wave of souls hovers in the distance. Somehow I'm in two places.

Vern pulls my left arm, and it lifts in the camp and wherever Oscar is. "We've gotta get out of here."

"Damn you," Oscar complains. "No moving. Stitches will rip."

Stitches?

I close my left eye, then my right, then my left, trying to judge what's happening between the camp and Oscar.

Margery says, "Is he back yet?" Now she's so close, I can count her nose hairs.

"Limited consciousness and movement in his short arm," Oscar says.

Short arm?

Then Oscar adds, "His heart beats every ten seconds as before."

I smile. "I'm alive." My voice echoes.

"Kid, we've gotta go," Vern says. "Demons and another wave of souls are movin' in."

"Gotta go. Demons," I say.

Margery flicks ashes onto my forehead. "What's he doing?"

"He is with Vern," Oscar says. "Must send Barry back there so he remains motionless."

"What? How'd he find Vern?" Margery's in a panic and her orange hair bobs in the background. "That bastard better not tell Barry anything."

Oscar squeezes a gelatinous liquid in my mouth.

Margery reaches for his wrist, but she's too late to stop him.

The bitter potion drizzles down the back of my throat. I gag and swallow.

"You idiot," Margery's voice fades.

Chapter 31

V ERN SHAKES me.

The camp comes back into full focus. A wave of orange souls and two demons close in. They snort out steam that smells like a sewage treatment plant.

I jump to my feet.

We run, Vern taking the lead.

We're slow at first, but accelerate to a crazy speed. If the sound barrier can be broken in Hell, we're breaking it. Millions of souls part into streaks of purples, blues and grays. A bitter cold wind whips into us.

Vern slows and I trip over him. The two of us tumble over each other until we come to a stop. My head sways and I struggle to catch my breath, each inhale a gulp of arctic air. "I can't be…" I pant and spit out pink flesh. "…this out of shape."

Vern's down on his hands and knees. He heaves up green bile and spits chunks of tar from his lungs. "Have you…forgotten…where… we are?" He tries to get up, but his hand slips. He lands face first in his sickening vomit.

I laugh, but it hurts so bad I hold my side and fight the urge to throw up too.

"Not funny." He wipes the goo off his face with the back of his hand and flings bile in my direction. It misses and hits a charcoal-colored wall that towers as high as the eye can see and stretches horizontally just as far.

This part of the refugee camp is a hellish world apart from the last place. Far dimmer and gloomier in both look and feel. The whole place is in shades of gray, including Vern and me. Dark silhouettes of faceless souls fidget with their hands while they wander among each other. Some run at the wall in a fury and adhere momentarily in a cartoonish pose. Then they peel off and slide to the ground. Others moan and claw upwards against the smooth surface, only to be pulled away and replaced by the forlorn figures behind them.

"Hell's beyond that wall," Vern says. "They're trying to break in."

I point upward at the infinite wall. "They think they can climb over that?"

"This is where the deceitful ones congregate. They know they belong in Hell. That's why they're trying to get in," he says. "I like this place because everyone has something to hide and keeps mostly to themselves."

There's another reason he likes this place. He's more deceitful than the lot of them. Still fresh in my mind is Margery's worry that he might tell me something she doesn't want me to know. Is she talking about the sacrifice, or is there something else?

I tense up. My fist clenches and crosses over Vern's jaw. Maybe it's this place working on my last nerve, along with being played for a sucker since I became a courier. My strength has somehow intensified in the camp. Vern flies backward into the wall and sticks like glue to it. He's out cold and limp, his head and torso bend forward. His legs dangle in mid-air.

With Vern passed out, the souls close in on us, their arms extended. I shove them back, but there are too many of them. It's like being in a zombie horde, only they're not hungry. They force us against the wall to form a ladder into Hell.

Vern wakes up and waves his arms. "Get off, you bastards!"

The souls back off, and I take a deep breath.

The wall groans and sucks Vern further into it. I take a hold of Vern's arms and he lurches forward at the same time. "Don't let them take me inside," he says. I try to pull him free, but he's merged in too deeply.

"Not yet." I pull harder. "I need to know more about the plan."

Vern's eyes widen.

"Don't play dumb. I know there's more than the child sacrifice." I get in his face and bare my teeth. "If you want to redeem even an ounce of your soul, you'll spill your guts."

The wall sucks Vern further inward. All that's poking out are his head, two arms, and the toes on one foot.

Damn. If he disappears, I'm screwed. I grunt, dig in, and tug as hard as I can.

"It hurts, kid. Let me go. There's no stoppin' me from gettin' sucked in."

I release him and slap his face. "C'mon, Vern, you owe me. What else is Margery hiding?"

"I don't owe you nothing," he says, "but I owe Marge less."

"Then tell me." When I slap him a second time, his bad comb-over falls onto his face.

Vern spits greasy strands of hair out of his mouth. "I can't."

The wall groans and creaks. It swallows what's left of Vern's extremities. He's nothing but a charcoal gray face on the wall.

"Vern!" I grab his nose and pull, then poke him in the eye.

"Stop it! I'll tell you." His breath labors. "There are no kids. She used the story about the child sacrifice to get you to lure the white warriors to the hole. They're what she's really sacrificin'."

I turn my back to Vern, clench a fist, and grind it into the palm of my other hand. "Stupid," I mumble. I'm so stupid.

I spin around and punch Vern the rest of the way into the wall.

The souls close in.

Chapter 32

A BLURRY SMEAR of orange hair atop a shriveled face hovers over me. "Hey, idiot. Wake up." Margery drills the tip of her cigarette into my chest.

"Damn it, bitch," I say with a scratchy throat. The burn is nothing compared to the feeling that I've swallowed a cheese grater. And while I'm relieved to be back from the camp, Margery's the last face I want to see.

"Keep still," Oscar says from the seat beside the cot where I lay. He's rubbing a cold salve on my neck that smells like rotted fish. When he leans backward, a bare, overhead lightbulb shines in my eyes.

I squint. "Turn that off, will ya?"

"No." He gives me one of his stern stares. "It is the only light in here."

Margery pushes Oscar aside and gets back in my face. "You had to go and miss the turn and put us behind schedule."

While I'd like to tell her to go fuck herself, I glare at her and bite my tongue instead.

Margery snorts like a bull and moves in closer. "What'd Vern have to say?"

"Nothing."

"Liar." Margery's eyes turn black. "Tell me what he told you or I'll rip that head back off!" Her fingers stretch like rubber and reach for my neck.

Oscar rolls his chair between us and knocks her to the side. "Let me fix him first."

A vision of Vern being sucked into the hellwall replays in my mind. I grit my teeth at the thought of Margery lying about the child sacrifice. Of taking advantage of my sympathy. Of getting me to lure the white warriors to the hellhole. I'll be damned if I tell her what I know, no matter what torture she inflicts on me. "He told me about the child sacrifice, you sick witch."

"Ha. Don't you think I already know he told you that? What else did he tell you?"

Shit. "Nothing."

She bares her teeth, saliva building around her mouth. "Liar."

That's hilarious, Margery calling me a liar. I squint and shrug my shoulders. "I swear. He told me nothing."

"Keep him here," she tells Oscar and rushes toward the exit. She kicks the door open and stomps outside in a cloud of smoke.

No chance I'm sticking around. I scan the room for the quickest escape route. This place is an old wood paneled shack, maybe three hundred square feet. Machine parts, fishing gear and rusty hand tools in the background. The door Margery used is the only way out.

Oscar wraps a bandage around my neck. "How do you stay one step ahead of her?"

"How's getting my head bitten off staying one step ahead?"

"Couriers cannot lose their heads and live, yet here you are. You went to the refugee camp and met up with Vern, who told you more about the sacrifice than you admitted to."

How am I supposed to know why any of that happened. I've been a courier for only a few days. I sit up. "I've got to get out of here."

"Slow down." Oscar pushes on my chest. "Reattaching your head a second time will be much trickier."

I try to push him away, but something's missing. "My arm! Where's my arm?"

"Have you forgotten the hellhound ate it?" Oscar reaches inside the armhole of my t-shirt and pulls out an infant-sized limb. It flops at my side.

My mouth drops open. Now I know what he meant by small arm when I was in the camp. I swivel my shoulders and it flails and slaps my chest. "What the hell? I can't control it."

"It will remain useless for some time while it grows, but you should have some ability to move it," Oscar says as if it's no big deal. "Visualize making a fist."

"Visualize?" I cock my head and do as he suggests. At first, my pectoral muscle and shoulder are all that move. I grit my teeth and try harder until my fingers wiggle. Then finally, my hand clenches into a fist and stays that way. I let out a loud breath. "How long will it take to grow back?"

"Should be normal by morning, but the muscles will remain weak much longer." He reaches over and loosens my fingers.

My heart skips a beat. "I can't wait that long."

"Next time, think before taking on a hellhound," he says matter-of-factly.

"Like that was my decision?" I look closer at my miniature arm and curl my lip in disgust.

"Any pain?" Oscar asks.

"No."

He almost looks disappointed as he says, "That means the salve is working."

"I do feel lightheaded. Is that normal?"

"Possibly a blood clot." He moves in close to my neck, lifts the bandage, and examines the cut.

My body sways, and my good hand grasps the side of the cot. "Whoa, there it is again."

Oscar rolls his chair backward as the room rattles. "You mean the earthquake?"

I frown. "That was an earthquake?" A screwdriver drops from above and lands between my legs. I wince and look up, then roll off the cot and onto the floor in time to avoid a hammer to the crotch.

When the ground stills, Oscar helps me to my feet. "That was the coal mine's ventilation system," he says.

"Coal mine?"

"No sense in playing stupid. I know everything."

Trisha and the white warriors. A panic electrifies my body down to the bone. "The Gates of Hell closed already?"

Oscar rolls his eyes. "You never listen. The tunnels that lead to the hellhole are caving in as your angel's apprentice friend near the Gates of Hell."

My face reddens. He does know everything. How?

Oscar walks to the opposite corner of the shack and I follow him. Fishing poles, handheld nets, tackle and other outdoor gear hang from the wall and ceiling. He reaches for a harpoon in the corner and pulls strands of cobwebs out with it. He holds the harpoon out horizontally and pushes it toward my face. "Take it."

I clutch the harpoon near the center, where a rope hangs and collects for fifty plus feet on the floor between us. It's heavier than it looks. "What am I supposed to do with this?"

"Use it on me," he says. "Then run. Take the path behind the shack. Follow until you reach two burial mounds ten feet high. They will be hard to see in the dark. Walk between them through a portal off the ranch. It leads to the highway."

"What are you talking about?" A strange feeling churns in my stomach. A cross between confusion and savagery. Part of me wonders why he's helping me. The other part finds it disconcerting that I'd hurt anyone, even if it is Oscar.

Oscar steps forward. He's one of the few men tall enough to get in my face. "I help you and you complain?" The wrinkles between his eyebrows deepen. "Would you rather wait for Margery to come back?"

"You expect me to believe you're helping me escape?" I twirl the harpoon until it's vertical, then hold it at my side.

"If it were up to me, you would still be headless. But it is not. There are other forces, good forces who want you alive."

"Are you telling me you're a double agent?"

Oscar curls his lip. "There will be someone waiting for you outside the portal."

"I'm not leaving Nina behind." Not to mention skipping out on Trisha and the white warriors. Maybe a few days ago I'd run away like a coward. Not now. Not knowing Margery has something lethal planned to take out the white warriors.

"I want Nina gone as much as you wish to save her, but I am in a better position to get her off this ranch." He lifts the tip of the harpoon up to his stomach. "Stab me."

My neck jerks back. "As much as I'd like to hurt you, I don't see the point."

"Must look like you overpowered me to get away."

"So you really are helping me escape?" Something's not right about this, but why complain if he's letting me walk out the door. Then again, he could be sending me into another trap, but I'll take that risk.

"No more talk." Oscar puffs out his chest and clutches tight on the neck of the harpoon. He grits his teeth, leans his stomach into the spearhead, and growls through the pain. When he yanks it back out, the barb tears out a hunk of flesh and intestine. Red meat falls to the floor. Oscar kicks it to the side, leaving behind a smear of blood.

"Damn." I wince and bite my tongue. The guy's tougher than I'll ever be.

"Now go save yourself." Oscar drops to his knees, holding in his guts. His breath labors as he continues to speak. "I will be fine."

Chapter 33

I STAND AT a fork in the dirt road. A churning in my gut urges me to follow Oscar's course, run down the path to the right, get far away from Margery, her magical cigarettes, and this hellish operation. But I'd never forgive myself if I did. There's also no guarantee he's truly sending me to safety.

Screw Oscar. I dart down the other road, hoping it leads to the hellhole. Like back in the refugee camp, I move as fast as lightning. All feeling in my legs is lost.

Shit!

Afraid of where I'll end up, I go limp to decelerate. Only I end up somersaulting in midair. My stomach drops and so do I, right off a cliff. I land on my stomach in a patch of dirt. All the wind expels from my lungs.

I lean to one side and spit out a foul mix of sour vomit and blood. The after-effects of a speedy run on Earth are no less harsh than in Hell's refugee camp. I turn over onto my back and suck air.

Of all the superheroes in all the comic books, Hell has granted me the superpowers of *The Flash*. I try to laugh but cough instead. Given a choice, I'd be Batman. Though *Hellboy* seems more appropriate. Then again, acquiring a superpower from Hell is useless if I wish for death every time I use it.

I sit up and look around. There's no telling my location or how close I am to Margery and the Gates of Hell.

Off to my right, there's rustling from a cluster of sagebrush. I hold extra still and sniff the air. *Sulfur*. That and a fiery orange glow gives away the hellhound's position.

I look skyward and mouth, "Cut a guy a break."

The hellhound leaps into the air and lands twenty feet from where I lay. Part of the bush protrudes from one side of its mouth. On closer look, whatever the beast is drooling over is not a branch.

The hound is gnawing on what's left of my arm.

I make a fist with my baby hand—a laughable threat. The bastard won't take another one of my limbs. "Drop it," I call out, as if the hellhound is a trained dog.

The hellhound grins and shows off its three-inch long canines, but it does what it's told. Its tail swings around and pushes my limb closer to me.

On second thought, I should've let the beast keep my arm. It's stripped of most of the meat with teeth marks nicked across the bone. One of the fingers and the thumb are still intact. My stomach would turn if it weren't already in knots from the run.

'Throw something at it,' I remember Margery saying. Even though I'm still skeptical it will do any good, I keep my eyes on the hellhound and search the loose dirt with my good hand until my fingers rake over wet, sticky tissue. I curl my lip and pick up my dead limb with my thumb and index finger.

As I stand, another quake hits. I stumble and fall on my ass.

The hellhound jumps up and down. A sinkhole opens between us.

I crawl backward as it expands, holding tightly onto my dead limb until I'm backed up against a wall of bedrock. My spine stiffens against sharp rock as I prepare to fall into the dark abyss.

Luck's finally on my side when the ground calms. I take deep breaths and shiver at the sight of the two-foot ledge that holds me. Carefully, I hug the wall and step sideways to safer ground.

The hellhound's head tilts. It watches my every movement. My guess, it's waiting for me to reach safe ground so it can feast on a few more of my limbs.

The toothy monster jumps and rushes my direction. My heart leaps and I freeze at first, then I throw the limb in the hole. The moron jumps in after his chew toy and disappears into the darkness.

That was way too easy. I pause, half expecting the hound to pop back out like a jack in the box. Instead, a cloud of dust rises out of the darkness. The tension in my body melts away.

A familiar voice resonates from the sinkhole. "Keep moving forward," Trisha says. "I'll take care of the hellhound."

Muffled responses echo along with hers, followed by the unmistakable sound of a sword unsheathing. I twitch with each hack and grunt and screech.

I call down into the darkness, "Trisha." There's no answer so I call for her again.

"Barry?" she calls back.

"Get out of there," I shout at the same time the ground begins to shake. The edge of the pit crumbles like sand in an hourglass. I jerk backward and yell, "It's a trap," over and over again. My voice trembles as much as the earthquake.

When the tremor settles, I call out, "Trisha."

No answer.

"Trisha!"

Still no answer.

I throw up my good arm and flip the bird to the heavens. "I'm on your side."

Damnit. There's no telling if she heard any of my warnings. *Now what?* I scan the area. Darkness behind me and a glow ahead. My only hope is it's the hellhole?

I climb up on the ledge that I summersaulted off of earlier. From higher ground I see floodlights, less than a quarter mile away. A white box truck is parked nearby. Black bodies, that must be demons, scurry around. In the center of it all sits a pump jack used to drill oil.

If I can make it to the hole, I have one last chance to warn Trisha and her warriors. Of course, the chances of me getting past Margery are slim, but I have to try.

I take off at a jog toward the site, hoping I don't land in Margery's lap.

Chapter 34

OUTSIDE THE circle of floodlights, I drop to my stomach and hide among tufts of tall grass. Dirt fills my nostrils, blown in from gusts of wind that rush across the dry ground. I breathe a sigh of relief that I crept in unnoticed.

Margery paces around the pump jack that sits center-stage. The thing is rusted out and couldn't possibly pull a drop of oil out of the ground. It can't serve any purpose other than camouflage for the hellhole.

A demon walks around from the rear of the box truck. He carries two rusted oil drums, one on each shoulder. So that's what we brought out here. What could possibly be in them?

If I remember mythical characters correctly, he could be a Minotaur, built like a bodybuilder and at least as tall as me. He's black as night, except for yellow, glowing eyes and sharp, bone-colored horns on his head. If there are many more of his kind lurking, I'm screwed.

Margery points at the demon. "Bruno, take those to the hole."

While I watch him do as he's told, I wonder what happened to the truck I was driving. Then I lift my torso, look at my new limb, and think maybe I don't want to know.

At least my arm has doubled in size. It's even more moveable than Oscar had predicted, but it's still useless against a demon. I close my fingers into a fist and shake my head at the lack of strength.

Bruno drops the barrels to the ground. They crash into each other with a thud.

Margery runs to the drums and steadies them with her foot. "If those open, we're toast!" She throws a cigarette at Bruno, but he ducks and runs back to the truck before he's hit.

The way Margery's reacting, a hellhound is less dangerous than the cargo we transported. What the hell's in those barrels that presents such a threat to the white warriors and to Margery and her crew?

Margery bugles like an elk and two more identical demons come into view from outside the circle of lights. She and the demons push the pump jack to one side, exposing a black spot at least six feet in diameter.

This has to be the hellhole. I don't know what I'd expected to see, but I'm surprised there's so little working machinery here.

I've been tortured by cigarettes, lost my head and arm to a hellhound, and have taken a trip to the refugee camp. Jumping into the hole to warn Trisha can't be much worse.

I scan the area and count five demons, plus one Margery. Where's Nina? I hold in my breath, squint, and study the darkness.

Still no Nina.

If Margery hurts her, or worse yet, beheads her…

Bruno makes his way along the side of the truck. He's carrying only one barrel this time. He hands it to another demon. Three more of them form an assembly line. Carefully, they hand each barrel to the next demon and place them beside the pump jack.

The ground starts to shake. The demons stumble and fall to the ground, their top-heavy weight throwing them off balance. It's like the earthquake scrambles their brains and turns them into every synonym for stupid.

I laugh out loud, then cover my mouth.

Bruno bugles and points my direction.

"What are you waiting for?" Margery hollers. "Go get him!"

I lay flat and fix my eyes on the demons. Not the brightest move, but I'm not leaving without warning Trisha.

Bruno leaps ten feet into the air and lands beside me. His size-twenty-four feet kick up a cloud of dust. He grabs the back of my pants, lifts me off the ground like a suitcase, and carries me into the light.

"Ow ow ow," I cry until Bruno drops me beside Margery. I cough, stand back up, and pull the wedgie out of my butt crack.

The passenger side door on the truck slams. Everyone's heads turn at the same time.

Nina runs toward us. She's a mess: blouse ripped to shreds, a shoe missing, dirt smeared across her face, and knotted strands of hair have fallen out of her ponytail.

"Bear!" She leaps into my arms. Her dry lips peck my cheek. She whispers, "Get out of here. Gita says the warriors are too close. You can't stop Margery."

Despite her violet, demon-possessed eyes, this is the Nina I know and love. I embrace her like I never want to let go. "Are you okay?"

"Don't worry about me." Nina pushes at my chest. "Put me down and I'll distract the demons so you can get away."

I put her down, and Nina's top falls to one side. I stroke her bare shoulder. "I'm not throwing you to the wolves again."

What is it with everyone wanting me to run away?

"I thought I told you to stay in the truck." Margery's airborne cigarette interrupts our moment, but it falls short. The old bat's losing her touch.

"No. Stay with Barry." Nina pulls her top further off her shoulder and glances in the direction of the five drooling demons. She winks and blows a kiss to the crowd. If this is her diversion, it's working.

It's also pissing off Margery, who's dragging hard on a fresh cigarette. She turns to Bruno. "Take him back to Oscar's shack before he screws something else up."

Nina takes off running and all the demons chase after her, including Bruno.

Now's my chance. I run toward the hellhole, dodging barrels, and drop to my knees. "Trisha, it's a trap! The white warriors are the sacrifice!"

Trisha, get out of there!"

"Get away from that hole." There's no mistaking Margery's baritone voice.

I'm ready to jump in when I hear Nina scream. I turn.

Margery has grown to fourteen feet tall, twice her usual demon size, and she's naked. I turn up my lip and fight not to close my eyes. She holds Nina upside down, a leg in each hand. "Get away from that hole or I'll make a wish with your girlfriend."

When I stand back up, I'm hit from behind. Not hard enough to knock me out, but my knees buckle and I'm seeing stars. One of the demons grabs me by my short arm and pulls me further away from the hole. My jeans scrape against dirt while I blink to regain my senses.

"Get him on his feet," Margery says. She holds Nina at her waist in one hand now. "How close are the warriors to the hellhole, Girlie?"

"I don't know." Nina pushes at Margery's thumb to loosen her grip.

Flames shoot out of Margery's head. "I'm asking your demon."

"I not tell you either." Nina comically raises her fists as if to pick a fight.

"Tell me or the demons pop your boyfriend like a giant zit."

A Minotaur takes my head between his gigantic hands. I gasp when he squeezes to drive the point.

"Ahhhh!" I kick backward against the demon's shin and he loosens his grip. "Don't tell her. Don't tell her."

Nina looks at me with puppy eyes. She hangs her head and says, "Through to the hole when the ground shakes next."

"Excellent." Margery drops Nina and turns to Bruno. "Get her back in the truck and keep her there."

Bruno flashes a mouthful of sharp, yellow teeth as he rushes Nina.

"Get away from her!" I lunge and struggle to get away and help her, but the demons hold me too tightly.

"Please, no. I'll go by myself." Nina jumps to her feet and takes off running. Bruno follows with his arms out.

Once Nina's in the truck, Bruno tries to open the door, but Nina's locked it. That doesn't mean she's safe.

"Time to close this hole and save the world, boys." Margery lets out a sarcastic laugh. "Get the lids off the barrels." She takes off toward the hole, losing height with each step until she's back to her seven-foot demon self.

Three of the demons rush in. The one who wanted to pop my head still holds me. They stand around the hole, ripping the lids off the drums to reveal a harmless looking milky substance.

"Don't spill it on the ground!" Margery reminds them. She turns to me. "It's only right you get to see what you made possible. You followed through perfectly, Honey, sending the white warriors to save children that don't exist. And you thought you were so clever, stealing my maps and meeting with Trisha behind my back. Funny thing is I left them there for you to find. The fact that ditsy Nina found them amazes me." Margery takes a few drags off her cigarette.

"I'm not taking credit for this," I tell her, both my fists tightly clenched. "You're in charge and this is the second time the Gates have closed on your watch."

"Ha. Hell has no use for a worthless human who sells his soul into servitude. The CEO always takes the side of his demons." Margery moves in close and gets in my face. She fights not to laugh as she adds, "God will be more pissed when He finds out what you've done to His holy army. You have no one to defend you."

I stand still, trying to comprehend the magnitude of what she's done to me. To figure my way out of this seems impossible.

The ground rumbles. Margery turns to the demons, points her finger at the hole, and calls out, "Dump the barrels."

Two of the demons tip their barrels. The milky white liquid pours into the hole. The third throws an entire barrel into the pit.

I fight against the demon holding my arms. "Trisha, it's a trap." I smash my heel into his foot, but the thing doesn't flinch.

"Direct hit." Margery cackles as she moves in closer to the hellhole. "Faster. Get all of the barrels in the pit."

A low hum rises out of the hellhole, intensifying in pitch and volume until it's discernible as screams.

Rage wells inside me as the demons continue to empty the barrels into the pit and I realize Nina was right. There's nothing I can do to stop this.

The hole erupts with the force of a thousand bats escaping their cave. Trisha ascends first, followed by a dozen or more warriors. Twenty feet above the ground, the warriors' wings freeze in place. Their bodies stiffen like statues. Trisha watches helplessly as they shatter like glass in midair.

The demons stop their work and look skyward while white shards rain down on their heads. The thought of the same thing happening to the white warriors in the hellhole is horrifying.

"Trisha!" I call out.

She flies toward me, stops, and hovers. Her eyes glow. "You idiot," she says. "You've ruined me." She soars higher, leaving behind a tail of bright light that explodes like fireworks on the fourth of July. All that remains is a message that sparkles in the night sky, 'fuck you'.

Margery stands by, looking into the sky, delighted by the message. "Those traitor bastards got what they deserve."

I rock back and forth and whisper a selfish apology. *God help Trisha. Please forgive me. It's not my fault.*

Another tremor starts and one of the demons loses his balance. The drum he's carrying tips to the side. The milky liquid spills on his legs and the ground. It creeps over his feet and up his legs, turning him into a statue. Too bad for Margery, the substance works equally against the powers of good and evil.

I feel the vibration in my feet. It works upward and into my bones. Weak in the knees, I brace my legs. The demon holding me feels it too. He loosens his grip, and I'm able to push him away. He's too top-heavy to maintain balance and falls to the ground.

"Stop pouring that crap," Margery calls out, but the earthquake tips two more canisters into the hole along with a demon.

I take off in the direction of the truck. "Nina!" I call out.

She opens the passenger door, but Bruno is lurking. He rushes around the truck, grabs Nina around the waist, and bugles as he runs away with her.

The ground cracks and separates in front of me. White ooze expands too wide to scale over to reach Nina. My nose burns from whatever is in the lethal substance. I run in a circle, trying to figure out where to go, but careful not to make contact with any of the ooze. All I see is defeat. At this point I'll be lucky to save myself.

One of the demons jumps at me and when it lands, the ground cracks. The newly formed white pool swallows the idiot.

I scan the area. Margery's a hundred or more feet away. When our eyes meet, she bugles. More demons appear out of the darkness, and it's obvious I'm their target.

Cracks continue to open: some inches wide, some feet wide. The ooze spreads like tree roots branching out. If I don't get out of here now, I'll be a statue like the rest of them.

If ever I needed my newfound talent for speed it's now. I look down at my feet and say, "Take me to the highway portal." There's no telling if direct orders will take me where I want to go, but it's worth a try.

I flip the demons the bird and take off, like lightening, down the only clear path, leaving them all in my dust, but guilty I've left Nina behind.

Chapter 35

Istop, drop and roll near the two giant burial mounds at the exit portal. On my hands and knees, I puke my guts up again. A plus that my feet took me where I wanted to go. A negative that the more I use my superpower the more my insides are torn apart.

I pick myself up, stumble between the mounds and end up in a ditch off the highway. Red and white lights, both northbound and southbound, stretch as far as the eye can see. Vehicles are at a standstill, some on the road, some in the median, some in the ditch. The strong smell of exhaust invades my nose.

People wander outside their cars, undoubtedly upset by the earthquakes. Some stand alone, others gather for support. They have no idea what really happened. That we're in the middle of a supernatural disaster, or that minutes ago their world was saved by a shape-shifting, chain-smoking demon. Teeth clenched, I shiver at the thought of the last few hours.

I turn around and the mounds are gone. If I weren't a coward I might rush back through the portal and stand up to Margery. Of course, I'd last about five minutes before she took my head, and I ended up back in the refugee camp with Vern. This portal could be useful in the future. I dig a hole with my heel to mark the spot.

My internal compass tells me the warehouse is to my left. I zig zag through the gridlock to the other side of the highway. A nearby sign verifies that I'm seven miles south of Trinidad.

My stomach's in knots, more so for leaving Nina behind than the run. A walk back to the warehouse will clear my head and give me a chance to figure out how to rescue Nina. Devising a plan to kill Margery would be an added bonus.

A horn honks behind me.

I ignore it.

It honks again.

This time I turn around.

A Hummer approaches, half in the dirt and half in the median. A man's voice calls out from inside the vehicle. "You all right?"

I don't answer, and instead veer farther off road, walking around a rest-stop sign.

The engine revs to keep up. He calls out again, "Barry, you want a ride?"

The last time a stranger knew my name, my life was turned upside down and inside out. I flip him the bird and pick up speed.

The Hummer continues to follow. The guy's not giving up. "C'mon, Barry. I'm the guy Oscar told you to meet."

I pause and think how I could collapse at any minute from exhaustion. Otherwise I'd take off running again. A ride would get me where I'm going quicker.

I turn my head and look through the passenger side window. "Why would I trust anyone who works with that bastard?"

"He works for me, and he hates Margery as much as we do," he says. "Trust me, I'm here to help you."

Considering how she treats Oscar, I can believe him.

Then he adds, "Margery and Vern set me up for the closing of the Gates twenty years ago."

Damn. I lean in the window. "And…"

"You're already wanted in Hell." He pauses like he's waiting for me to react.

I sigh.

"Son, you can get in this vehicle or take your chances against Satan's demon bounty hunters."

I take my chances and get in the Hummer.

We continue off road and pick up speed. He holds out his hand to shake. "Name's Pete."

I turn my head and look out the passenger side window. Last thing I want is to let another person or being into my life who will end up screwing me over.

As traffic thins, he forces his way onto the highway and says, "That whole quake was pretty damn crazy, huh? I almost got out of my vehicle. Then I remembered I'm driving this thing, and figured I can drive anywhere." He laughs.

I force a laugh and not my head. If only he knew what it was like to be at the epicenter. "Listen, I appreciate the ride, but I'm not in the mood for conversation. Drop me off at the Highway 12 exit, and I'll be on my way."

He clears his throat. "I was just trying to make you feel comfortable and maybe take away some of your guilt for letting Margery fool you."

"Stop the vehicle." I reach for the door handle and yank on it, but the door won't open. "Damn it. Let me out."

"I wouldn't do that if I were you. We're driving kind of fast now. Road rash is a painful recovery whether you're mortal or immortal."

"I'd rather have a red ass than listen to your bullshit."

He laughs. "Sorry. I really am here to help you."

I snap back, "I don't need anyone's help."

"Of course you do," he says. "What would you say if I told you I can release Margery's control over you. Well most of it."

At this point I'm not buying anything the guy is telling me, but I have to ask, "Who are you?"

Pete turns on the interior light. He leans toward me and widens his eyes. They're bright violet, like Oscar's and Nina's.

"You're possessed?" I jerk away from him and lean against the door.

"It's okay. My demon's dormant."

"Margery just set me up for closing the Gates of Hell. Excuse me if I'm a little on edge."

"Understandable," Pete says while he nods his head.

"Your demon's still in you?"

"Yeah, but you're talking to me, Pete, not a demon," he says then shifts the conversation. "Twenty years ago, the last time there were similar earthquakes, Vern tried to blame me for closing the Gates of Hell. He was even successful for a while. That alone is a reason to trust me."

"No shit?" I shift back center seat, but I'm skeptical the guy is trustworthy like he says.

"Vern, Oscar and I helped Margery start her operation after World War II. Vern and I were buddies for a lot of years."

"You know he's dead, killed by an angel's apprentice." I don't tell him about Vern and the refugee camp, but I'm sure he'd appreciate him being sucked into the wall to Hell.

Pete laughs. "Damn. I never thought Trisha would ever catch up to that greasy bastard."

"Who do you work for? Please don't say Trisha."

"Me a white warrior? Hell no. I don't have a thousand years to chase vans," he says. "I save drivers from Margery just like the apprentices do, but I give them back a life. A few stick around and work for me."

"I don't get why Oscar sent you to pick me up."

"Like I said, Oscar works for me before Margery. You're right, the guy hates you, but he'd help you despite his feelings because of who you are."

Curious, I lean in and ask, "What do you mean?".

"I'm here to help you because…well, there's no nicer way to say this, son. You're fucked. Satan's already released a couple hundred bounty hunter demons to bring you down to Hell."

"You already told me that." I suck in my bottom lip, bite down and think how he's scaring the shit out of me.

Pete goes on to say, "Bounty hunter demons are the least of your worries. Those earthquakes released your father from his tomb out near the Great Sand Dunes."

"My father? Ha. I don't have a father."

"Everyone has a father and yours happens to be the fallen angel, Azael."

"You expect me to believe my father is a fallen angel?" I think about my only knowledge of my father. The man who came to my mother in the night and bewitched her by singing *Can't Get Enough of Your Love Baby*. She named me Barry White Frost as a constant reminder to never have sex again. Now I find out the story was literal. I have to laugh.

"Not so funny. You're only the second person besides Hitler in the entire history of man to alienate both God and Satan at the same time."

I sit quiet—speechless. Even my thoughts are frozen.

"For now, you're best off with me. I'm taking you back to my safe house. You'll eat and sleep, and in the morning I'll release you from Margery's power."

"Seriously? You can do that?"

"Yes, and as soon as you're free, you'll help me hunt down your father and eliminate him from existence once and for all."

I nod my head, but I'll be damned if I'll follow this guy's orders. Once he breaks my contract, I'll ditch the guy, get Nina away from Margery, and we'll never be seen again.

The End

TURN THE PAGE TO READ A PREVIEW OF
WARRANT FOR DAMNATION
BOOK 2 OF ANGELS DARK AND DUMB

Warrant for Damnation

Book 2 Preview

Chapter 1

Wʜᴏ ɪɴ his right mind goes home with a stranger he met on the highway like I did last night? Then again, it's not the stupidest thing I've done over the past four days.

I peek outside the bedroom where I've tossed and turned the last few hours. At nearly five in the morning, the second-floor hallway is deserted. Perfect for a speedy getaway. But there's no telling who or what lurks behind the oak doors that break up the flowery red-and-gold wallpaper.

On an ordinary workday, I'd rush off to my courier job for Hell. Yes, the literal Hell. Then I'd spend half my day pissing off my demon boss Margery, although not on purpose.

No work today though. As of yesterday, life is…*complicated*.

While I'm innocent, Margery managed to convince Satan that I sabotaged his plan to open the Gates of Hell. And God believes I sacrificed hundreds of His white warriors to get the job done. Worst of all, Margery's Minotaurs took off with my friend Nina before we were able to escape together.

Floorboards creak under my skater shoes as I duck into the hallway, my messy brown curls brushing under the doorframe. The smell of pancakes rises from the first floor and awakens my senses in a bad way. Fruity flavored cereal and gin are more my breakfast of champions, but it doesn't matter. No time to eat. I've got to sneak out and save Nina from the seven levels of misery that Margery's likely inflicting on her.

A doorknob clicks to my left.

Damn!

Pete exits a bedroom with a smile. "Morning, Barry. Able to sleep?"

He's the stranger who brought me to this old farmhouse, and he'll try to convince me to stay. Pete professes to be a miracle worker for the Catholic Church and can smooth things over with God. He's also promised to nullify my contract with Satan and provide protection against Hell's bounty hunters. Boy, I want to believe him, but the mosh pit of butterflies in my stomach warn to trust no one.

My grip tightens on the wood-carved railing. *Get out. Find Nina.*

On impulse, my feet take off, descending the stairs at hyper-speed, as if I'm *The Flash* in the comic book series. Unable to control this ability attained during a trip to Hell's refugee camp, all I can do is tuck and go into a double somersault to put on the brakes. I land on something rigid at the bottom of the staircase, pain erupting in my ribs.

"Damn!" I shiver at the sight of a wooden shard from the broken coat rack piercing my t-shirt and torso at my side. I grit my teeth, grab the protruding spike, and yank. Cupping the gash is no help. Bright red blood oozes between my fingers and drips onto my baggy jeans.

Seems everything I do lately turns to shit or a fountain of gore.

Pete descends to the first floor, my body twitching with each heavy step of his cowboy boots. He's more wrinkled than I remember. Maybe his jet-black pompadour concealed his age.

He sweeps back his tan tweed jacket and slides a thumb into the front pocket of his jeans. The way he dresses, the guy could be a cowboy professor.

"I'd ask how you feel," he says, "but that wound is answer enough."

While struggling to pick up my glasses and stand on unsteady legs, I clench my jaw tighter and suck air between my teeth.

"Hold on, Barry." Pete skips down the last few steps. "Let me help."

Still clutching my ribs, I recoil, suspicious of anything he's offering. "It'll heal in a few minutes."

"Let's at least get you tidied up," he says, "and into clean clothes."

"Thanks, but no time." I face the front door, decorated with panes of yellow-stained glass. "Besides, I shouldn't be here. I have to find Nina before Margery turns her into a demon chew toy." My gaze drops, knowing what a gutless loser I am for leaving her behind.

"Two seconds outside and you'll have Hell's bounty hunters fighting to take you in for closing the hellhole. At least stick around long enough to break your contract with Satan. They won't be able to track you."

"You saw me move. I'm too fast to catch."

"But not very coordinated." He lifts an eyebrow and half grins.

After a brief pause, I sidestep toward the door.

"Nina's fine." Pete pulls a cell phone from his blazer pocket. "Oscar's keeping an eye on her at the warehouse. Call him. He'll let you talk to her."

"He hates me, not to mention he's Margery's lackey."

"Like I told you. Oscar's a double agent. He's been feeding me information for years and has always been reliable." Pete waves the phone. "Go ahead. His number's the last incoming call."

I blow out a long sigh, reach for the cell, and grasp it with blood-soaked fingers. Instead of contacting Oscar, I flip through the call log and find the names of people close to me. I glare at Pete, feeling more guarded than ever. "Why've you been talking to my mother and Father Timothy?"

"She's worried…" he stutters. "They're worried, Barry, and I've been watching—"

"Watching Margery take my soul and turn me into a wanted man."

"Remember last night, when I mentioned Margery blamed me for closing the Gates of Hell the year you were born? I understand what you're going through. It's why you should stay. Barry, please, there's so much more you need to know."

The phone slips out of my hand and falls to the floor. My only thought, *No one can be trusted, not even Mom.*

I'm out the door at hyper-speed, my side erupting with pain.

Chapter 2

No surprise, my speedy feet take me to the deserted break area outside Margery's Southern Colorado warehouse. They have a way of knowing where I need to be, so it's a given that Nina's nearby.

I drop to my knees and barf stomach acid across the patio: a thing that happens after a run, brought on by strobing lights and absolute terror during a trip. Then again, being this close to my demon boss is equally sickening. Whatever the cause, I'll never get used to it.

I wipe my mouth with the back of my hand. Saliva trails to where I rub the string off on my jeans, inches below my crusted wound. As much as my torso still burns, I'm more focused on Nina. She's probably inside, massaging Margery's smelly feet and splintered toenails. The thought makes the nausea linger.

The dawn glows in the sky, and a cool summer breeze sweeps through the trees and over my arms, raising the hairs. Then the sight of two vintage soda machines against the rusty warehouse wall sends the chill along my spine. If only they'd serve a cold drink to wash away the nasty coating on my tongue. Instead, they dispense the spiny essence of a demon through a direct connect to Hell. The very ones Margery uses to possess and control her workers.

While I escaped that fate, Nina did not. A reminder the demon that possesses her may be an obstacle to leaving this place.

Off to the left, a tall figure in red coveralls rounds the corner, approaches a broken picnic table, and brushes against sunflowers that grow between cracks in the concrete. A salt-and-pepper braid rests near a nametag that reads "Oscar."

When he sees me, his high cheekbones, brown weathered complexion, and turned-down mouth express his usual stoic mood and equal irritation that I'm here.

"You gonna tattle to Pete?" I sneer at him, annoyed that Oscar's a double agent for good and evil. But I'm also relieved he's not Margery.

He removes a flip phone from his pocket, and in a deep, monotone voice says, "While I would enjoy seeing you suffer at the hands of Margery, I will tattle to Pete, as you say."

"Where's Nina?" I step toward him, but my foot catches on a crack, driving me headfirst into his jutted chest. It's like head butting a light pole.

"If it were not for Pete, I would launch you to the moon." Oscar's way of reminding me there's only one thing upon which we agree. We hate each other.

I straighten my bloody shirt, step close to his face, and burp the words, "Where is she?" Considering he's nearly tall enough to look me straight in the eye, he got a full dose of my sour breath.

"Such a fool. You cannot win this contest." His expression contorts as he releases a loud fart.

"What did you eat?" I fan searing nostrils.

"Fermented eggs." Oscar pulls a plastic bag from his pocket. Inside, the putrid snack has been bitten through to a black yolk. "Counteracts Margery's diarrhea curse when she is unsatisfied with my work. Want one?"

"Hell no." After the tortures I've witnessed the evil bitch inflict upon him, he'll need at least a dozen after Nina and I escape.

"Suit yourself." Oscar shoves the bag into his pocket, speed-dials the flip phone, and places it beside his ear. A few seconds later, he says, "Yes, Pete, the fool has arrived."

I yank away the antiquated cell. "Call off your mole. I'm not leaving without Nina."

"Fine." The line goes silent. "Bring her back to the boarding house. We'll protect you both."

Having no actual plan on where to take Nina, his offer is tempting. And we're better off with him than anywhere else. "Full disclosure on everything?"

"That was my intent before you left," he says. "It's time you know about your father, your birth, your purpose."

Oscar turns his attention to where he entered, then lifts his chin and sniffs the air.

My stomach drops as I pull the phone away from my ear. There's no denying that odor.

Cigarette smoke.

Chapter 3

"Look who's here." Margery trounces around the corner wearing an orange Bronco's t-shirt, shiny blue spandex pants, and black flat shoes. She tosses a smoldering butt at Oscar, landing a hex over his heart with an electrical surge.

Oscar's face stiffens, but the tough bastard remains silent, hiding the pain she's inflicted, as he always does. A thing about him I respect.

In a gruff New York accent, Margery asks, "Did I hear Barry right? My most trusted employee is working with Pete?"

I flip the phone closed and slip it into my pocket. This is bad. What will Pete do when he finds out I've exposed his informant? And what else will Margery do to punish Oscar?

Rather than confirm her suspicions, I call out, "If you need to torture someone, torture me."

"Why? You deserve a doggie treat for crawling back to expose this traitor." Margery winks an eye smeared with black liner and turns up an evil grin that exposes nicotine-stained teeth. A few days ago, the sight of her wrinkled mug and flaming troll doll hair made me want to piss my pants. Today, I'm fighting the urge to wring her neck.

"Not a chance I'm crawling back... to you!"

"What other choice do you have, Honey? God and Satan are out to get you." She holds up a hand, magically flips another lit cigarette out of thin air, and explodes into a mixed cackle and emphysema cough.

"Only because of you." I think how stupid I was to fall into her trap. To let her set me up for closing the Gates of Hell.

Two short and scrawny dudes wearing red hoodies and jeans round the building with their heads covered, making them difficult to see in the emerging morning light. Nina's the last to stumble into view. Her long, blond hair dances in the breeze, and her slender body swims in a pair of red coveralls with the sleeves and pant legs rolled up.

I lock onto her violet eyes, a side-effect of being possessed by a demon. When she smiles, my heart races. Thank God she's okay. But when I wave her over, her lips purse and she shakes her head. Must be her demon responding, or more likely she's terrified.

Margery's back on Oscar, flicking successive cigarettes at him like a sharpshooter. "How long have you been helping Pete?" He stumbles backward with each hit but stays on his feet. Her sadistic curse fuses his mouth, and his lips disappear. It's obvious she's not expecting a response. I would know. She's done the same to me.

Oscar's white socks come into view, noticeable as his uniform shrinks in size. Unzipping his suit provides no relief from her next punishment, a full body wedgie.

"Stop it!" Saliva spews from my mouth. This is all my fault, but what can I do?

"Don't worry, Honey." She snorts. "If I hadn't chopped off his balls years ago, he'd be in more pain."

The fabric's alive, squeezing Oscar's arms and legs until he falls like timber, the back of his head hitting the concrete. Unfortunately, he remains conscious, his blaming eyes narrowing in on me as he grunts.

If I were him, I'd cry out in agony. For Oscar, this is torture *du jour*. It's probably why he was so selfless in feeding information to Pete. I was wrong about him. No matter how much we loathe each other, his suffering makes me want to destroy the demon bitch ever more.

Real flames sprout and toss around Margery's upturned hairdo as she narrows a cigarette butt on me. "Get your ass in the warehouse. The only place you're going is to the Great Sand Dunes Park to bow to Azael."

My thoughts flash back to last night, when the hellhole quaked and erupted with the remains of sacrificed white warriors. Pete said the Earth's vibrations released a fallen angel by the name of Azael from his Blanca Peak tomb in the Sangre De Cristo Mountains. He insisted I'm his son.

"How do you know Azael's loose?" I ask.

"Who do you think helped him escape?" She smirks. "Honey, he's your father and my creator, making old Margery your big sister."

Nina gasps.

And my mouth gapes. I'm half shocked and half confused by her confession. Being the spawn of a fallen angel is hard enough to believe. Sharing my origin with a demon of her caliber is downright mind-blowing.

Margery snaps her fingers below my chin. "What, no smartass comeback? This is a first."

"Bullshit."

"If you've been talking to Pete, there's no way that asshole hasn't spilled the beans about your father, although he's unaware of my kinship. That's been a well-kept secret."

"We are not siblings." With a clenched jaw, I stare down at her.

"Listen, dumbass, I'm a demon, and you're Nephilim. My mother's a volcano. Your mother's a human. Regardless, we share the same maker. Our allegiance belongs to Azael." Margery draws on her cigarette and releases the smoke through her nose. "You can't deny our connection. Four days ago you begged me for a job. Yesterday we plugged up the hellhole to release Azael. Today you exposed this traitor." She twists the cherry on cigarette's smoldering butt into Oscar's forehead, putting it out and causing him to convulse.

"Sto, stop," I stutter, wishing there was something I could do. The sympathetic expression on Nina's face says she's feeling the same.

"Oh, Honey, I haven't even gotten started."

"Why did you have me sign a contract to work for Satan?" I ask, more to distract her from Oscar.

"Insurance," Margery says. "Everything I did, from courier contract to ensuring your warrant for damnation, was to guarantee you won't stray from Azael. You can't run to the CEO of Hell because Satan thinks *you* stopped the Gates of Hell from opening. And you can't run to God because He thinks *you* sacrificed part of Heaven's army. Now you're only safe with Old Margery."

"Safe…with you? *Ha!*" And she's reminding me how ridiculous it is that Satan insists he's the CEO of Hell, modernizing the underworld into a profitable corporation.

"God especially loathes your kind," Margery says. "Somehow, you're the only Nephilim who hasn't been hunted down and destroyed since the time of Noah, although I've yet to figure out why. Bottom line, you're stuck with me if you want to live.

A lightbulb goes off, realizing she ostensibly worked for Hell, but she's been faithful to an entombed fallen angel all along. A being who expects my loyalty after a sperm donation.

"Seemed impossible a dud like you could have escaped the hellhole last night." Margery mouths a fresh cigarette. "Let me guess. Oscar led you to Pete."

Not wanting to make things worse for him, I keep quiet and don't confirm she's guessed right again.

"Don't be naïve about Pete, Honey." Margery's eyes pulsate and spiral, so I look away or risk becoming hypnotized. "Has he admitted to re-imprisoning Azael on the day you were born? He deprived you of your father and rightful upbringing. If it weren't for Pete, you'd be at Azael's side, ruling over humankind. Instead, you grew up a loser."

While standing over her with arms crossed, I think how this is nuts. Everyone expects me to blindly be a part of *their* grand scheme. Again, it seems as if Nina and I are better off on our own.

"I get it." Phlegm gurgles in her throat as she says, "You're pissed about being set up. Get over it. Had to be done. Now take Blondie into the warehouse unless you prefer to watch the skaks finish off the traitor."

The hooded men hover over Oscar's motionless body. They uncover their heads and stare at each other, appearing unsure of Margery's intent. With shriveled skin and sunken cheeks, they belong in an Egyptian mummy exhibit. More horrifying, their receding lips bare cone-shaped teeth resembling those of a tiger fish.

"What are they?" I swallow hard.

"I told you. Skaks. Couriers I've been incubating in the sand dunes for the last half century. They're what happens when Old Margery and a hellhound spit in their graves. Unfortunately, they emerge as idiots." She approaches the skaks, her long bulbous fingers pushing them toward Oscar. "What are you waiting for? Use those teeth."

"Margery… they can't eat him." I rub the back of my neck and search for a way to stop the looming predators.

"It's their purpose, Honey. They'll feast their way through every human who denies your father's rule."

In an instant, a skak dives at Oscar's throat, ripping through his neck. His decapitated head rolls to the side, mouth gaping and tongue protruding.

With wide eyes, Nina screeches. Afraid she might bolt, I wave her over, but she replies by mouthing, "No."

On hands and knees, the monsters feast. Blood splatters across the patio. Intestines twist and twirl before being sucked in like spaghetti noodles.

My mind floods with regret. If I had stayed at the boarding house. If I had never met Margery. If a fallen angel hadn't claimed me as his son. Oscar would be alive.

Something inside me snaps. I rush the demon bitch, enveloping her hands. My grip locks around her fists with insane determination to rip off her hands so she can never throw another cursed cigarette. But electrical surges shoot along my forearms, and my palms burn as if I'm holding hot irons.

"Get him off me! Get him off me!" Margery's eyes turn black.

When no one comes to her aid, her fingers enlarge and nails morph into talons. I'm launched backward and bust my tailbone against a soda machine. The demon dispenser is knocked off balance, teetering to the ground with a loud crash. The machine's lights flicker despite it being unplugged.

Quickly, I roll away. This is the worst possible time for an evil essence to slither through the dispenser and take up residence along my spine.

"Bear!" Nina screams my nickname, a sign she's in control of her demon. She races over and yank my arm to help me up.

"We're getting out of here," I say. "I have a safe place for us to go."

This time, she agrees.

I spit on scorched palms. The pain's excruciating, but less distracting than Margery staring at her swollen talons with a stunned expression. Her flaming hair fizzles to sparks, and when she flicks her hand, only a puff of smoke releases.

Resembling a toddler in full tantrum, she jumps up and down. "Where…are…my…cigs?" Her wrinkles stretch and transform into black scales until she's a reptilian monster, stomping toward us, barking, "Get them."

With little to nothing left of Oscar but bones, the skaks are quick to attention, setting their sights on us being their dessert course. I grab Nina around the waist, throw her over my shoulder, and take off like *The Flash*.

Chapter 4

T HIS TIME my sprint sputters to a stop as if I'm running out of gas. And Nina's missing from my arms.

What the hell?

I scan the surrounding dry grass and rocky terrain before spotting her twenty yards in the distance, at the side of the dirt road.

"Nina!"

Upon approach, one of the legs on her coveralls is shredded. She's immobile and unresponsive; a bloody streak reveals the extent of her wound.

Not only did I drop her, I dragged her. I hurt her bad.

Please be okay, please be okay.

My hands tremble as I yank my t-shirt over my head and wrap it around her leg where the flesh has been scraped to the bone, from hip to knee. But it's a worthless bandage.

What now?

While stroking her arm, I search for ways to help her without jeopardizing other body parts.

Pete.

I fumble in my pocket for the flip phone, then find the last number in the call history. After one ring, he answers. "Almost there. I know where you are."

"How?"

"GPS tracker on the cell." He blows out a loud sigh. "I would never leave you high and dry with Margery."

Reflecting on the trouble I've caused over the past twenty-four hours, how could I blame him if he did?

To the east, Pete's Hummer comes into view amid a cloud of dust. But within seconds, squawking off to the west drowns out the racing motor. A familiar flock of crows, the size of eagles, approaches. A few days ago, they protected me from God's army. I doubt it's their intent today.

Uncertain who will reach us first, I scoop up Nina's limp body, careful not to slip on the pool of blood. I hurry toward the Hummer, hoping I don't shift into hyper-speed and drag her again.

A few yards short of the vehicle, the black birds win the race, swooping in, wings whipping across my shoulders. Claws tear. Beaks peck. I swear they're gulping chunks of my flesh, possibly their way of taking me to Hell in pieces. All I can do is bear the pain and keep the pace.

Pete plows through the murder of crows and brakes to meet us. Through the cracked window, he yells, "Hurry! Put the girl inside!"

No shit!

I struggle to open the back door and place Nina onto the seat, but a wing knocks me off my feet and sends my glasses flying onto her stomach.

"Get in!" Pete says.

"I'm trying!" My arms flail, fighting off birds, but there are just too many. I'm about to take shelter beneath the vehicle when my hands glow and sting. Sparks shoot from my palms, and a bird bursts into a puff of smoke.

"Whoa."

Feathers fly everywhere and stick to the blood coating my chest. The others squawk, ascend, and hover.

I chuckle at the sight of a bent cigarette wedged in my palm.

Found your cigs, Margery.

I throw it at a crow in a nosedive, taking advantage of my pause. The bird freezes mid-flight, his eyes bulging from their sockets before he explodes like his brother.

Wow.

While pointing my palms skyward to hold them at bay, I climb into the back seat.

"Hang on." Pete flips a U-turn.

The crows follow and strike, one after another, rocking the vehicle.

"What," I say, "no protection spell on the Hummer?"

"Yes, but I suspect your active contract with Satan and your warrant for damnation are more powerful." His head bobs as he struggles to see past the flock swarming the windshield. "Cross your fingers they don't lift us off the ground."

"Open the sunroof." I lean between the front seats.

"Are you nuts? The crows will do anything to collect your bounty." He points at a white feather hanging from the rearview mirror. "A few strokes of that and Trisha will fly in with her white warriors."

"Trisha's warriors are dead… sacrificed—"

"Not all of them."

"Good to know, but I can get rid of the crows faster," I say because she's the only one I fear more than God and the CEO of Hell.

"You sure?"

"Yes. Trust me."

"Okay," Pete says, sounding unconvinced when he pushes a button on the dash.

The sunroof slides open, and I stick my hands through the slot, quick to aim my glowing palms skyward. As I twist through the window, each cigarette discharges with a sting that intensifies. After slaying a quarter of the flock, the remaining birds circle west and out of sight.

I collapse against the seat, feeling tarred and feathered.

"How did you repel the crows?" Pete asks. "What were those sparks?"

"Cigarettes," I say while unwrapping my shirt to check Nina's wound. She's healing but slowly. "Somehow, I absorbed Margery's cursed cigarettes."

"You what?"

"I'll show you later." With Nina resting on my lap, I wrap a nearby blanket around her motionless body and place my glasses over the bridge of my nose. "Nina's unresponsive. Will she be alright?"

"She's a courier. As long as her head is attached, she's alive." He peers over his shoulder. "Is she breathing?"

I lower my face to her nose but feel no breath on my cheek. Nor is her chest rising and falling. "No."

"Give her mouth-to-mouth," he says. "If she goes too long without oxygen, she'll go insane, and there's no curing crazy in a courier except through beheading."

Nina's gone through enough. If she loses her mind too…

While replacing her breath, I think how this is an unfortunate way for our lips to meet again.

"Candy," Pete says into his phone. "We're ten minutes out. Nina's with us and she's hurt. Tell Ulla and Inez to prepare for skin regeneration, and worst case, a decapitation."

BUY *WARRANT FOR DAMNATION*
BY WINNIE JEAN HOWARD
AND READ MORE

About the Author

Winnie Jean Howard (a.k.a Mean Winnie Jean) writes dark humor for all ages. Her main focus is creating action-packed stories that are quick reads.

While born in Chicago, today she lives near Denver, Colorado with her ever growing family. She enjoys hiking with her husband and beagle, drinks way too much wine, and watches way too many zombie movies. In fact, she's a bit addicted to any form of media that aims to scare.

For over thirty years, she's been an IT geek, professional writer, and artist. She's also been involved in the development of anything from simple websites to network monitoring to space defense systems. Recently, she returned to school to add graphic designer to her list of careers. Besides fiction, she writes technical specifications, instructional manual, marketing articles, organizational newsletters, and much more. She's also the founder, Chief Editor and Creative Director over at ArmLin House Productions.

More About the Author

winniejeanhoward.com
facebook.com/winniejeanhoward
instagram.com/meanwinniejean
deviantart.com/meanwinniejean
tiktok.com/@meanwinniejean
twitter.com/meanwinniejean

About the Publisher

ArmLin House is a unique publisher and production company. We help you develop your story in a memoir, business book, instructional video, and more. Then we format your story and help you present your work, whether you release it yourself or we do it for you. And once your story is out there, we can help you promote it with written and visual aids.

It's our mission to help our clients succeed in whatever they do. We take your visions and make them possible through coaching and distribution assistance. The products we help produce are informational and entertaining, as well as help you market yourself and your business. We produce based on your needs, whether it be in print, digital, audio, or video formats. Then we help release it to a worldwide audience. .

Contact the Publisher
armlinhouse.com
facebook.com/armlinhouse
instagram/armlinhouse
twitter.com/armlinhouse